STARGATE
ATLANTIS™

THE WILD BLUE

MELISSA SCOTT

FANDEMONIUM BOOKS

An original publication of Fandemonium Ltd, produced under license from MGM Consumer Products.

Fandemonium Books
United Kingdom
Visit our website: www.stargatenovels.com

STARGATE
ATLANTIS™

METRO-GOLDWYN-MAYER Presents
STARGATE ATLANTIS™
JOE FLANIGAN RACHEL LUTTRELL JASON MOMOA JEWEL STAITE
ROBERT PICARDO and DAVID HEWLETT as Dr. McKay
Executive Producers BRAD WRIGHT & ROBERT C. COOPER
Created by BRAD WRIGHT & ROBERT C. COOPER

WWW.MGM.COM

Print ISBN: 978-1-905586-76-9 Ebook ISBN: 978-1-80070-061-1

CHAPTER ONE

THE SQUARE around the Stargate was crowded, or what passed for crowded on Sateda, the mid-week market just winding down. The biggest of the temporary stalls were still from off-world, Ronon saw, speculators looking for salvaged goods their own worlds couldn't quite make or maintain, but he was pleased to see that the goods offered in exchange were not just ordinary foodstuffs, but things worth almost the value of the salvage. Some of the Satedan stalls were offering food as well, great jugs of cold tea and little crisp cakes and even knobs of sugar-candy: more progress. The last time he had been in the capital, the provisional governor Ushan Cai was still requiring everyone to contribute all their rations to the common store. All the meals had been cooked and served communally, even while people were spreading out into the ruins.

Cai saw where he was looking, and nodded. "We're — doing better." His voice was that of a man who doesn't want to call down ill luck. "We've got a trade agreement with Varres now, food for scrap metal and technical assistance, so we don't have to be as tight as we were when we got here. Of course, when we started coming back, no one wanted to live away from the square."

In case the Wraith returned, Ronon knew, but guessed also that not many people had wanted to live too far from their fellow humans. Even now, the ruined city could seem painfully empty, as though the dead were just waiting to peer out a broken window, or step from a shattered door.

"Now we've got people in the houses all along Arkan Avenue,

and we've cleared the old rail line from the Souter Depot all the way in to the Gate Square."

"That's good."

"It's made it a lot easier to bring in coal —" Cai stopped abruptly as one of the women detached herself from a group around the notice board that had been erected beside the hotel's pump.

"Governor! Why are we still having power cuts? You said we'd get all day power as soon as we'd gathered enough coal, and the gods know there's solid ton of it ready now. I swear I carried enough of it."

"That coal's for the winter," Cai said.

"We're still hauling coal in every day, me and my boys and half the city." The woman put her hands on her hips, obviously aware of the people who had stopped to listen. The shortage of electricity was a long-standing grievance, Ronon knew. The borrowed Lantean generators went to power the hotel and the radio station and a handful of nearby buildings, things the Lanteans needed as much as the settlers. At the beginning, that had been enough to take care of everyone, but now that more and more Satedans were coming home, they were spreading out into buildings that couldn't be hooked up to that limited network. Cai and his people had rigged up a couple of coal-fired generators, but the coal had to be scavenged from depots and cellars all over the city, and everyone was acutely aware that there was only a limited supply available. "You could run the generators all day, and we'd be able to bring in more than enough coal to make up what you burn."

"We don't know that," Cai said, with more patience than Ronon could have mustered. "Marti, you and your boys have done an amazing job emptying the old rail depot coal storage — I didn't think we'd be finished before autumn, and

it's only just past midsummer, and most of that coal is here."
Marti relaxed slightly under his praise, and Cai went on, "But
you know as well as I do that there's not enough left to both
increase the hours we have electricity and have enough coal
to get us through the winter."

"We can't keep going like this," she said. "Two hours out
in the middle of the day, every day — anyone who's trying to
use a power tool has to stop and start, and it's just no good."

"I know," Cai said. "We're working on it, believe me."

"She's right," a man said. "Those breaks are just killing us.
Can't they come at the end of the day, or in the morning?"

"You can bring that up at the next citizens' council," Cai
said. "This was what worked best for most people the last
time we voted."

"Or you could let more people tie in to the Lantean grid,"
another man said. "They don't have any shortages."

"Again, that's a matter to bring up at the next council," Cai
answered. "And we'd need to bring the Lanteans in on it, it's
their technology. And if anyone finds another big coal dump
— and I'm sure there are some out there — we'll revisit the
question."

For a moment, Ronon thought they were going to keep
arguing, but Marti grinned.

"That's fair enough. We'll need to find more supplies for
next year anyway."

"You and your boys — and their cousins — you've done a
great job," Cai said warmly, and the crowd dissolved, people turning back to the business of packing up their stalls.
Ronon started to turn away, relieved, but Cai caught his elbow.
"Hang on, I'd like a word —"

He broke away as yet another man came up, saying something about the water supply, and Ronon let himself drift
toward the hotel entrance, where he knew Cai would end

up. This was exactly the sort of thing he didn't want to do, another secret, faintly guilty reason for not leaving Atlantis. Leave Atlantis, and he'd be stuck playing referee when no one was actually wrong, but there wasn't enough to go around. He'd rather be shot at any day.

It didn't take long for Cai to disengage, and he came up onto the hotel's porch, mopping his forehead with a handkerchief. "Warm day. Care for a beer, Dex?"

The beer wasn't what it used to be, but bad Satedan beer was better than most of what he could get off world. Ronon nodded with some enthusiasm, and let himself be steered to a corner table in what had been the hotel's lobby and was now the community's main meeting place. A teenage boy brought a pitcher and two glasses and scurried off.

"Well," Cai said. "You remember the Ezes?"

Ronon frowned, shaking his head.

"They managed to survive the culling up in the mountains around Escavera, them and seven or eight other country families, and a few months back Jana, that's the daughter, got the bright idea of walking to the capital to see if there was anything they could salvage. That was when your people were looking for Dr. Weir."

As always, being treated as one of the Lanteans felt odd, but Ronon just nodded. "Yeah. I think I heard something about that."

"Beron and the older girl, Vetra, they've gone back, but Jana's stayed to help Hocken with the mapping. And one of the things she said got me thinking. They came past the old hydro plant at the Narmoth Falls, camped there a couple of days after they got down the cliffs, and she said she didn't think it had taken any damage from the culling. If we could get that running again…"

"Yeah." The Narmoth Falls power plant was old and reliable

and close to the city, and it had been one of the main power sources before the culling. "You'd have to fix the power lines between here and there — and I'm not sure why you're telling me. I'm not an engineer."

"Neither am I," Cai said. "And neither is much of anybody here. I was hoping maybe somebody on Atlantis could help us out — at least to see if there's any chance this could work."

Ronon took another swallow of his beer. "I'll talk to Colonel Sheppard."

"Thank you," Cai said, and filled their cups again.

***

Mel Hocken taxied the Rapide into the hangar, then ducked back out through the side hatch, resting her hand affectionately on the fiberglass skin of the fuselage. She had shepherded the kit-built plane that she'd found and purchased for Governor Cai through complexities of getting it to Sateda, and then through the build and testing, and she was more than a little in love with the airplane. It wasn't anything like the F-302s she'd flown before she retired, but she'd always kept a general aviation license, and the Rapide had more than lived up to its marketing, especially after McKay had modified its engines to run off a scaled-down naquadah generator. Through the open door she could see Tarek Mav, the groundsman, turning the ox-drawn mowing machine onto the landing strip, the great blades whirring. That was typical of Pegasus, the mix of top-of-the-line technology and something that would have been out of date on Earth a hundred years ago, and she couldn't help shaking her head. It went along with kerosene lamps and an outhouse, having to walk for an hour to get to what passed for town, but she had known what she was getting into when she took the job. She'd put in her twenty years, and couldn't see a reason to stay, not anymore, but she hadn't had anything to go back to on Earth, either. Then Cai had offered this job, and as soon as the Rapide was fully approved, she'd be paid to train the first class of Satedan pilots, just as she'd trained the drone operators who were piloting the unmanned aircraft currently searching the areas north of the capital for any signs of survivors. Of course, at this point 'pay' was food and housing, and a promise of any profits made from the Rapide in the future, but she was, somewhat to her own surprise, perfectly content with that. Plus her Air Force pension was still going into a bank account, and she suspected the Atlantis crew would be willing to place orders for her if she needed anything, but all in all she couldn't see any reason to go home. She had no family there, and Sateda was wide open, a new frontier where her skills were genuinely needed.

The sound of the mower grew stronger again as Mav made another pass along the strip, and she pushed herself away from the plane. Before she reached the door, she heard clattering footsteps on the stairs that led to the drone station on the roof, and glanced back to see Yustyna Tan hurrying toward her.

"Mel! I'm glad I caught you. Something interesting's turned up."

"Yeah?" Mel climbed the stairs behind her, to emerge in the little shack they'd built on top of the trolley barn's roof. Eventually it would be the control tower for the field, or at least the base of a tower, but for now, with only the Rapide and three drones to worry about, it was filled with the monitors and consoles for the drones.

Cai had borrowed a couple of Air Force sergeants as trainers, and one of them was at the controls, frowning lightly as she studied her screens. One of the other Satedans, an ex-mechanic named Alpir Bas, was leaning over her shoulder, watching intently.

"What's up?" Mel asked, scanning the screens. They were filled with the tops of pine trees, more of the forest that lay between the capital and the Alduren Plateau, and she looked to the screen that superimposed the drone's position over a map of the area. The trouble was, the map dated from before the culling, and showed plenty of things that were no longer there, like the railroad that had once run north to the Narmoth Falls. The drone's last half hour of flight showed as a bright line, running along the edge of the area to be mapped and now turning back toward the west as though it was doubling back on its tracks.

"We spotted a clearing," the sergeant said. Her name was Montaigne, and she had a good reputation both as an operator and as a trainer. "I'm checking it out."

As she spoke, the trees in the video thinned out, and Montaigne reached for the controls to adjust the camera, zooming in on the cleared ground that suddenly appeared. "That looks man-made —"

She stopped, grimacing, as the ruins of a farmhouse slid into view, and the Satedans sighed in chorus. The roof had fallen in, though there didn't seem to be any signs of fire or explosive damage, and weeds and brush were beginning to choke out the fields.

"Looks like they were culled," Bas said, his voice tight, and Tan nodded.

"Or they abandoned the house," Montaigne said. "It looks more like the roof fell in than that somebody took it off. And the Wraith would use culling beams —"

"It doesn't really matter," Mel said, seeing the Satedans bristle. It was a knee-jerk reaction for them to assume that the Wraith had killed anyone who was missing, and they were weirdly offended if you suggested anything less. We'd rather the surprise was a good one, Tan had said, with her wry smile, and Mel could kind of understand that. "Let's mark it and move on."

"Yes, ma'am," Montaigne answered, her hands busy on the controls. The camera pulled back, the clearing receding, and the drone turned back to the north.

"That's not the only thing," Tan said. "There's something up here in this edge quadrant that looks interesting. At the end of the last pass, just before we made the turn back to the south, it looked like there might be something in the foothills of the Spur. I've got the images up on my screen if you want to see."

Mel nodded, leaning over her shoulder. The Spur was a line of mountains that ran south from the edge of the Alduren Plateau.

"It's not real clear," Tan said, "but it is… interesting." She had been a photographer before the Wraith attacked, and had taken to digital images like a duck to water.

Mel squinted at the screen, trying to figure out what she was seeing. Those lighter patches had to be rocks, the slopes of the Spur where it separated from the Plateau — it had been a mining area, Tan had said, though sadly it had been metals rather than the coal they needed for heating. And if those were rocks, then those other shapes must be low-growing brush, and that — it was too straight to be natural, surely? "There?"

She pointed, and Tan nodded. "Yes. This is an enhanced image, and it was at a funky angle because of the distance, but that looks almost like timbers to me. It might just be logs harvested before the culling, but I think it's worth checking out."

"Makes sense to me," Mel said. "Sergeant. Can we do it this run, or will we need to wait for the next mission?"

"This is my last pass for the day," Montaigne answered. "We're losing the light, and I'm toward the end of my fuel load anyway. I thought I'd make my turn to the east, see if I can't pick up a little better picture. But I definitely think it ought to be on the schedule for tomorrow."

"Sounds good," Mel said. She looked around the little room, seeing the reluctant hope in the Satedan faces. "It's definitely worth the look."

***

It was another bright day on Atlantis, and the sun had dried the platforms outside the mess hall. They hadn't even been frozen, Ronon thought. They were moving into Atlantis's summer, and now there were nights that didn't actually get cold enough to freeze: definitely an improvement over their previous location. He wished he could go for a run, sprinting along the catwalks and ramps that tied the towers together, but he was due at another briefing. He filled a cup of tea, and made his way into the meeting room.

Most of the others were there before him, Sheppard still looking uneasy at the head of the table, and Dr. Weir looking just as awkward sitting beside McKay and Zelenka. Teyla had brought coffee in a travel mug marked with a stylized head in the Americans' favorite red-white-and-blue, and as Ronon took his place beside her, Beckett came bustling in, spilling tea and apologies. Zelenka found a napkin, and Sheppard looked at his laptop.

"Right. The agenda."

Ronon leaned back as the others ran through the listed business, ignoring Teyla's reproving look. He didn't have anything to contribute to any of these topics — things were actually running pretty smoothly at the moment, though if the past was any indication, that should mean the Wraith or the Vanir or some other weird thing was going to show up and send everything straight to hell — and he waited patiently until they reached the end of the list.

"Ok," Sheppard said, a faint look of relief on his face. "Anybody got anything else to bring up?"

"Yeah," Ronon said, and saw a look of surprise on almost everyone's face. "Governor Cai asked me to ask something."

"Ok," Sheppard said again, and across the table Dr. Weir leaned forward with a look of genuine interest.

"The biggest problem they've got right now is electricity," Ronon said. "The capital used to be supplied from a hydro plant at the Narmoth Falls, here." He touched his tablet to bring up the file and projected it onto the main screen, then used his finger to circle the spot. "The people who walked down from Escavera came down from the Plateau there, and they said they didn't see very much damage. They weren't even sure the Wraith had been there. Cai wants to send a team up to see if they can get the plant going again, and he wanted me to ask if anyone on Atlantis would be available to assist his team."

"Don't look at me," McKay said. "I don't do that sort of thing."

"No one was," Sheppard said, not quite under his breath.

Zelenka quirked a smile. "What kind of a plant is it, do you know? What sort of drive for the generators?"

Ronon shrugged. "There were some sort of big turbines at the base of the falls, but that's all I know."

"I've seen similar plants," Zelenka said, to Sheppard. "And probably some of the other engineering staff have also. We could certainly take a look."

"What about helping them with repairs?" Elizabeth asked. "If that's what the governor has in mind?"

"I don't think he'd say no," Ronon answered, "but nothing's got that far yet."

"We don't exactly have a lot of spare parts lying around," McKay said, and Zelenka nodded.

"Rodney's right, we might be able to provide information, expertise, but — presumably they would need transmission cables to get electricity into the city, and that's not something we can supply."

"Perhaps there are still stocks of such things in the city," Teyla said. "They are hardly fragile, and the Wraith had no reason to destroy them. And it would improve conditions in the new settlement if they had electricity that was not dependent on our generators."

"We're getting a little ahead of ourselves, aren't we?" Sheppard asked.

Ronon shrugged. "We won't know till we take a look."

"How far is it to the — Narmoth Falls, you said?" Elizabeth frowned up at the map.

Ronon tried and failed to convert Satedan measurements to the Lanteans' kilometers. "Four or five days' walk. Maybe more, if the ground's bad. I was thinking we could borrow a puddle jumper. So that we don't waste anybody's time."

"Makes sense. Dr. Zelenka?" Sheppard looked down the table, and Zelenka shrugged.

"I will go, yes. And I will ask Dr. Kasper to come along, I think he's had some experience with similar technologies."

"All right." Sheppard closed his laptop. "Tell Cai we'll send a couple of advisors. But let's get this done quickly if we can — things are calm right now, but who knows how long that will last?"

Ronon nodded, and the meeting broke up. He made his way down to the control room to radio the message to Cai, and found Teyla at his side as he left the radio room.

"That is a good idea of Cai's," she said. She was determined to keep her fingers on the pulse of Atlantis's dealings with the locals. "Do you think it can be done?"

Ronon shrugged. "I'm not an engineer."

"But you have opinions." Teyla allowed herself a demure smile. "And you have talked to the ones who have seen the plant?"

"Cai talked to them," Ronon said. "He says they said there wasn't much damage in the outer buildings, just broken windows. But nobody's looked at the machinery in years."

"Then your group will be the first," she said, smiling.

***

Ronon could smell the machine shop a block away, oil and smoke and hot metal, and he stopped in the doorway, not wanting to interrupt the work at hand. The building had been part of the railyard before the Wraith came, and had survived remarkably unscathed. The returning settlers had cleared the main room and gotten the small forge working again, complete with the giant bellows to fan the fires. At the moment, they had a long piece of metal in the fire — it looked like a piece of rail — and a girl in a grimy shirt and pants was hauling rhythmically on the chains that moved the bellows while five or six men shifted the rail back and forth in the flames. Sparks rose from the bed of coals, and the leader lifted a hand.

"Now!"

The others heaved together, lifting the rail out of the fire and onto the concrete floor, hastily shifting it so that the heated section was against a thick wooden bollard. Two of the men began hitting one end with sledgehammers, while smoke began to curl up from the bollard. The girl who had been working the bellows ran for a couple of waiting pails of water, but the leader shook his head, and she poised, waiting. The rail began to bend, a gentle curve, the hammers falling faster, the noise deafening.

"Stop!" The leader dropped his hand, and the girl hastily threw the first pail of water over the smoking bollard. She reached for the second as the others hauled the rail away, then stopped as the smoke faded.

"Good job, boys," the leader called. "Let it cool now and then we'll measure."

The girl tapped his shoulder, jerking her head toward the door, and the man turned, his homely face breaking into a smile. Ronon smiled back, recognizing him: Vin had been one of the first wave of settlers. It was good to see him settling in.

"Dex! Good to see you!"

"You, too," Ronon said. They clasped hands, moving away from the heat of the forge, and Vin cocked his head.

"What brings you here? Anything I can do for you?"

"I hope so," Ronon answered. He grimaced as the girl began working the bellows again, sending another wave of heat across the room. "Mind if we step outside?"

"Not at all."

Ronon gave a sigh of relief as they moved out into the breeze, and Vin rummaged in his pocket for a grubby handkerchief and mopped his sweating face.

"So, what do you need?"

"Governor Cai is looking for a way to get reliable power back on in the city," Ronon answered. "So I'm looking for people who know about the Narmoth Falls power station." He outlined the plan quickly, Vin nodding eagerly, and finished, "I was hoping you might know some folks."

"Valiena Bar — she's the apprentice here — her brother was with the power company, I'm pretty sure," Vin said. "Cremer Pas wasn't at Narmoth Falls, but he worked on a similar plant over in Calianta. He's working salvage right now, but I think he's still in town. Val might know some more." He turned away without waiting for Ronon's response, sticking his head back into the workshop. "Val! Come here a minute, please."

The girl trotted over, wiping her face on a dirty sleeve. "Boss?"

Ronon explained quickly, and she nodded.

"My brother Atil worked for the power company all right, but he's out on a salvage job right now." Her face clouded. "He went out with Evrast Mar, but they haven't checked in for a few days."

"Evrast Mar?" Ronon frowned. The name was familiar, but he couldn't quite place it.

"General Mar, he was," Vin said. "Alpine Rangers. It's too bad he's already left; he was the guy I was going to send you to next. He's been up to the Spur a couple of times since he came back, he might know how things are at the Falls."

"If you're going up there," Bar said, "would you keep an eye out for my brother — for the General's party? They should have checked in by now."

"Radio reception's always tricky in the hills," Vin said, patting her shoulder.

"We'll definitely keep an eye out," Ronon said. "Anyone else you can think of who might know the power system?"

Vin gave him two more names, but when Ronon tracked them down where they were repairing one of the old town pumps, only one had actually worked on the system. But she had more names to offer, and by the end of the day he had a list of five people who had had some experience of the Narmoth Falls station. All had said they were willing to join the Lanteans to take a look at the plant — all the more so, Ronon guessed, because they'd be traveling by puddle jumper instead of hiking — and he made his way back to the communal dining hall in a cheerful mood. The supply situation had improved considerably, to the point that he felt no compunction about accepting Cai's invitation to join him for dinner. In fact, he admitted silently, leaning back to let one of the hall's runners set half a loaf of bread in front of him, it was a treat to eat Satedan food again.

He brought Cai up to speed on the day's researches and handed over the list of volunteers. Cai took it, frowning thoughtfully.

"Yes, I know most of them. I think we can spare three or four, if your people think that will be enough?"

"I'll have to ask Dr. Zelenka," Ronon began, and stopped, seeing Mel Hocken threading her way through the crowded tables.

Cai looked over his shoulder, and motioned for the Lantean woman to take a seat. "Trouble?"

"Not exactly." Mel slid onto the bench next to Ronon, nodding her thanks as the nearest runner brought her a glass of the smoky lemon tea. "We've picked up an anomaly."

"What sort of anomaly?" Cai asked.

"The drones picked up something at the very edge of their range," Mel said. "It might — and I stress might, because we can't get closer, and Yustyna's enhanced the picture as much as possible — show an artificial clearing and a structure, or at least cut timber."

"Where?" Cai leaned forward, his food forgotten.

Mel reached into her pocket, spread out a tattered map. Ronon recognized it as the kind tourists picked up to take them to the mountains, before the Wraith came. She turned it so that they could all see, and touched a spot on the far side of the ridge of mountains that came down off the Alduren Plateau. "Right about there."

"That's right in the middle of mining country," Ronon said.

Cai nodded. "We've always thought the people up there would have had warning when the Wraith came, and if they'd gone down into the mines — whole towns could have survived."

Ronon tilted his head to see more clearly. Narmoth Falls and its power station were on the western side of the Spur; the spot Mel indicated was on the eastern, not actually that far apart, except for the jagged ridge between them. The mines were mostly on the eastern side, where the slopes were less steep, and a rail line had run from there to the capital.

"We've been looking for a good reason to take the Rapide out on a proper test flight," Mel said, "and this looks like it to me. We can get there and back easily, and have plenty of time to circle and take pictures, see what's really there. We could take in the whole length of the Spur."

Cai hesitated. "I don't know. If anything goes wrong, it's a long way back to the field."

"It's always going to be a long way back," Mel said. She added, more moderately, "It looks to me as though there might be clearings on top of the plateau, and at the base of the Spur. We've got some fallbacks if we need them. And we're going to have to take the risk sometime."

She was right, Ronon thought, but he also understood Cai's hesitation. They had traded a lot of Sateda's wealth for that airplane; they couldn't afford to lose it and have nothing to show for the loss. "The highway used to run up to Narmoth Falls, didn't it?"

"That's right." Cai frowned.

"We're going up there," Ronon said, to Mel. "I'm taking some people up there to see if the power plant can be salvaged. What if we see if we can clear a length of the road for a landing strip? That way, if you had a problem, all you'd have to do was cross the Spur."

Mel nodded slowly. "I like that idea. And then if the plant gets going, we can make that a regular base, move north onto the Plateau —"

"Let's not get ahead of ourselves," Cai said. He stared at the map a moment longer, tapping his finger on the table, then shook his head. "All right. If you can get a landing strip open up there, then I'll agree to send the Rapide to look at that anomaly. If it is another settlement…" He shook his head. "Well. Too early to start thinking like that."

Ronon nodded, knowing everything Cai wasn't saying. The more of their own people they found alive, against all odds, the more it felt as though they were becoming Sateda again, and not just a collection of refugees. He cleared his throat. "Say, while you're up there — assuming you go, of course — there's a guy who went toward the Spur and apparently he's missed his radio check. Can you look for him as well?"

Mel shrugged. "It depends on how big a party he's got, and whether he wants to be found. But, sure, we can look."

"You're talking about Evrast Mar," Cai said.

Ronon nodded again. "Yeah."

"He was warned — everybody who goes into the back country is warned," Cai said. "We don't have the people to mount rescue missions if something goes wrong."

And that was also reasonable, Ronon thought, even if he guessed Cai didn't particularly like it. "He's done this a lot, right? Maybe he just dropped his radio or something. If we're up there, we might as well look."

Cai relaxed a little. "True enough. But first, let's see what's left of the highway."

CHAPTER TWO

IT WASN'T a long flight from the capital to the Narmoth Falls, and Radek was glad he had claimed a seat directly behind Lorne's co-pilot, Sergeant Fishman. The puddle jumper was crowded with the six members of the exploration team — the four Satedans plus Ronon, and Radek himself and Dr. Kasper — plus Lorne and two more military personnel. It was easy to see that this would be a long and tedious journey on foot: once they left the ruins of the suburbs, the gently rolling grass-land gave way to steeper hills and thicker forest. A road had been cut through it once, and he could see the remains of a rail line, but in far too many places, the trees had filled in, or a bridge had slumped into a stream. Arkad Pin, the Satedan engineer who had worked on a similar plant in a different province, leaned forward, frowning, and shrugged in answer to Radek's questioning look.

"The transmission lines ran along the rail cut. I don't see too many missing towers so far."

Radek looked again, and this time the sun was at the right angle to spark fire from the bare metal. The towers were low and crude compared to the ones in use on Earth, but would be sufficient for the job. "The actual wires are missing, I think."

Pin nodded. "Yeah. And they'll be a beast to replace if we have to haul cable by ox-cart — assuming we can even find some spare oxen."

"Not to mention replacement cable," the older of the two Satedan women said. Arkadya Kos, Radek remembered, and she had been an administrator for the power company before the Wraith came. She closed her eyes. "There was some stored at the plant, but most of it was in the city. I don't know if anyone's looked to see if it's still there."

"First things first," Kasper said. "There's no point wasting time on that if the turbines can't be repaired."

"But if they can," the younger Satedan woman, Valiena Bar, said, "we need to be prepared."

Radek tuned out the discussion and craned his neck to see out the windscreen. The edge of the plateau was just visible in the distance, chocolate-colored rock rising like a wall out of the forest. A stripe of white split the wall, resolving as they came closer into the foam of a waterfall. Presumably the buildings of the power station were at its base, but the trees still hid them from sight.

"Narmoth Falls," Ronon said. "The Narmoth River runs southeast to the Spur, then south along the mountains. Otherwise it would be an easy way to get supplies up here."

"That's too bad."

"Great rapids, though," Ronon offered. "My unit used to train there."

"If that's a thing you enjoy," Radek answered, and Ronon grinned.

"It weeded out the weak — what's that?"

"I see it," Lorne said, from the pilot's seat, and tipped the jumper into a slow turn that brought them back over the break in the trees. Radek realized he was holding his breath, and then released it in a sigh of disappointment as they passed over an empty meadow.

"Nothing, sir," the co-pilot said, and Lorne nodded.

"Sorry, folks."

"Thank you for checking," Pin said, but the Satedans' disappointment was almost palpable.

The trees thinned out as they got closer to the plateau, and for the first time Radek could see clearly what was left of the road. It reminded him sharply and unexpectedly of back roads around the SGC's Colorado Springs headquarters, two lanes running parallel to a double set of railroad tracks. The paving was in ruins, but the rails seemed surprisingly intact — certainly there was enough undamaged material that they could cannibalize one line to repair the other, Radek thought. And there were the transmission towers, too, short, sturdy rhomboids thrusting up out of the forest's edge. A few of them trailed lengths of cable, and the forest had grown in on others, but it looked as though this end of the system might be repairable.

They were coming up on the plateau itself now, and Lorne slowed and banked, giving them all a good view of the power plant nestled at the base of the falls. There were three main buildings, the largest closest to the base of the falls and two smaller ones to the west; they all had broken windows, and showed no signs of life, but the roofs seemed to be intact, doors closed tight against the weather. The rail lines ran along the western side of the clearing, fanning out to enter a set of low-slung barns, and there was what looked like a turntable outside one of them; there was a cluster of transmission towers as well, set behind a double fence that was beginning to fall apart.

"That little one was the superintendent's house," Kos said, "and the apartment for the staff was next to it."

And of course the largest building was the plant itself. Radek craned his neck again, trying to get a good look. Presumably the turbines had been set back into the wall of the plateau, where they would have direct access to the stream; certainly there was enough water coming off the plateau to drive more than one. If they could get this working again, it would solve the capital's power problems for decades to come. No wonder Cai had wanted them to make the attempt.

Lorne set them down outside the main building, and they climbed out, stretching after the long flight.

"Let's take a quick look in the plant," Radek said, "make sure there are no deal-breakers before the major leaves us."

"An excellent idea." Matthias Kasper nodded. He was one of the older scientists on Atlantis, didn't travel much off world, but he'd worked on hydroelectric plants as a young man, and Radek thought his experience would be invaluable.

"Go ahead," Ronon said. "We'll check the dormitory."

"Ms. Kos?" Kasper began, but she had already joined them, rummaging in the carryall she had slung over her shoulder.

"I'm ready."

"And I," Pin said.

Radek nodded, and started for the plant.

The main door was unlocked, swinging loosely on its hinges. It opened onto a broad lobby, its brightly tiled floor drifted with dirt and leaves. There was also the remains of a fire, ash and half-burnt bits of broken furniture, left over, Radek thought, from the Eze family's stay. Pin made a small, unhappy sound.

"The offices are upstairs. The control room and the generators are through there." Kos pointed to a set of double doors marked with a muscular arm holding a stylized lightning bolt. There were words below it in Satedan script: the name of the plant, Radek guessed.

"Control room first," he said, and started for the door.

It was locked, of course, and he swore under his breath. "Mr. Pin —"

"I have a key," Kos said quickly. "At least, this should be a master —" She fumbled it into the lock as she spoke, and smiled with relief as the tumblers clicked back. "There."

"Well done," Kasper said, and flicked on his flashlight.

Radek did the same, letting the circle of light play over the

walls. Here in the working sections of the plant, there was
less decoration, though the walls had been painted a vivid,
cheerful yellow that was now peeling in strips from the plas-
ter beneath. They were in a long hall lined with what looked
like offices, each one with a forest-green door set with a large
pane of pebbled glass marked with the arm and lightning
bolt and more Satedan words.

"Workers' rep, junior director, hydrologist, another junior
director…" Pin's voice trailed off, and he shook his head.
"This way."

There was another locked door at the end of the hall,
but Kos's bundle of keys opened that as well. They stepped
through into an antechamber with metal stairs rising to either
side and a room full of consoles ahead of them. Windows set
high into the walls near the ceiling let in a murky light, but
Radek swung his flashlight methodically across the space
before moving forward. He could hear a distant deep rumble, and guessed it was the falls.

"This is the main control room?"

"Yes," Kos said. He could hear the echo of the efficient sec-
retary she had been, the pride at having everything at her fin-
gertips. "The technicians monitored the turbines from the
floor, and the supervisors were on the mezzanine, behind us."

Radek nodded, turning to look up at the open balcony
above him, then let his flashlight play across the consoles
again. Everything was dark, of course, but he saw almost no
damage, no broken glass, no shattered screens, no torn and
trailing wires.

"They were supposed to do a controlled shut-down," Kos
said. "If the Wraith came. That was company procedure. Shut
everything down and leave it so that it could be restarted cold.
They were supposed to cover the consoles and then get out."

"I think they did a good job," Pin said. "From the way the

switches are set — it was all deliberate."

"Good," Radek said. "So far, so good. But we still need to look at the turbines."

"Through here." Kos led them through the consoles to a door set in the right-hand wall. It was heavier than the others, with a bar dropped across it as well as the locks, and Radek had to help Pin lift it out of its brackets before Kos could open the locks. She pulled the door back against the wall, fastening it in place with a heavy hook, and raised her voice to be heard over the sudden roar of water. "The generator room."

Radek nodded, playing his light across the cavernous space. Kasper joined him, and they moved from one generator to the next. There were four, all silent; the first three had been switched to standby and then decoupled from the system, while the fourth had its side open as though someone had been working on it when the Wraith came. The exposed parts showed signs of rust and mineral deposits, but the others seemed to be in decent shape.

"They cut the grid power when the Wraith came," Pin said. "Everybody went to generators — well, everybody who had them."

"The policy was to protect the station," Kos said. "We'd been culled before, and once the Wraith were gone, it was important to get the power back to as many people as possible. Only this time…"

Only this time, it hadn't been a culling, but an all-out attack, an attempt to destroy the Satedans as a people. And by the time it was over, there had been no one left to restore the power, and no one left to use it. Radek cleared his throat, looking at Kasper. "I think the technicians did their jobs. It looks as though there's a decent chance we could get this running."

"I have not worked on a system precisely like this," Kasper

said, "but I think it's close enough. The water can be switched
— through here? From the falls, I mean."

"That console controls the intake gates," Kos said. "And
there are manual failsafes as well."

Pin moved toward a panel set into the wall to the right. "At
Gerilon, where I worked, we had an internal generator, just
for internal system —"

"We had one, too," Kos began. "Oh, you've found it."

"Yes, and it looks as though everything was shut down
correctly." Pin turned his own flashlight on the panel, and
Radek came to join him.

"It has its own turbine?" All the switches were turned off,
and a metal grill had been drawn across the controls, as
though the technicians might appear at any moment. It was
like looking at some of the Ancient ruins, Radek thought,
that same haunted sense of missing time, people made viv-
idly present by their absence.

Pin nodded. "If we can get it running, we'll be able to
power the station buildings."

Radek put aside his thoughts. "All right. Let's get back to
the others and tell them so."

***

Ronon left the other Satedans to scout through the superintendent's house and the dormitory, and walked back toward
the jumper. It had landed on the cracked pavement in front of
the power plant, and the remains of the road stretched back
toward the distant capital. Lorne came to meet him, resting
his folded arms on the stock of his P90.

"What do you think, can they get this working?"

Ronon shrugged. "Depends on how the plant workers
left it."

"It would be nice to get lucky."

"Yeah." Ronon shaded his eyes, trying to gauge the length

of the pavement. "Do you fly those little planes? Like Colonel Hocken?"

"I'm not really a pilot," Lorne said. "I'm just a guy with the ATA gene. Why?"

"Cai wanted us to see if she could land the plane up here if there was an emergency. One of the drones spotted something on the other side of the Spur, and she wanted to take a look."

"Maybe?" Lorne glanced over his shoulder. "Sergeant Fishman! We're going to take a look at this road."

They made their way along the tarred strip, Ronon scuffing idly at the loose pebbles that had worked loose from the surface. There were plenty of cracks, and grass sprouted through many of them, but fewer potholes than he had expected — though of course there had been no wheeled traffic on this road for a decade. The snow had come and gone, but there had been no trucks or carts to damage the frozen surfaces. A few clumps of saplings encroached on the edges of the paving, but they would be easy enough to remove. They had done more damage to the rail line on its raised bed, tucked closer against the edge of the forest. The bank had washed away in places, cross-ties jumbled on top of each other, the rails spanning a gap twice as long as a man's arm. They weren't going to get the trains running again anytime soon, Ronon thought, and that meant Hocken's airplane was more important than ever.

"How long a road does she need?"

Lorne turned to look back at the power plant, already receding into the distance. "The minimum distance for the Rapide is something like 1500 feet, and we've probably got twice that to the edge of the clearing. The question is whether the surface is safe, and if she's comfortable clearing the trees and those towers."

Ronon turned in a full circle, scanning their surroundings. The transmission towers were on the edge of the clearing opposite the rail line, and to his eyes, they looked well clear of the road. Most of them trailed strands of cable, though only a couple of lines still connected one tower to another. "I don't think the wings are any wider than this road."

"Yeah." Lorne reached into his pocket and pulled out a camera, began slowly panning around the clearing. As the lens passed him, Ronon resisted the urge to grin and wave.

"When you give that to her, tell her we can clear out all those little trees. I don't think there's much we can do to even out the surface, but I'll talk to Zelenka if she needs that."

"Air Force people land on worse every day," Lorne said, with a shrug. "The Rapide's supposed to handle bush flying."

"It'll be her call," Ronon said.

By the time Lorne had finished filming the road and the space around it, the other Satedans had begun to set up camp in the lobby of the power plant.

"Not the dorms?" Lorne asked, stowing his camera, and the sergeant, Fishman, shook his head.

"They — there wasn't time to take anything. They're still full of people's stuff."

Ronon grunted agreement. Even when he'd been a Runner, he'd hated having to camp in the wreckage of other people's lives; he'd taken their belongings in order to survive, but it had never felt entirely right. Lorne nodded, too, and Fishman said, "Anyway, better to have everybody in the same place, just in case."

In case of what was a good question, Ronon thought, considering they hadn't seen any signs of life on the flight up, but there was no point in taking chances. The Eze family and their neighbors had survived up on the Plateau, and there were bound to be others. Anyone who'd survived the culling was likely to shoot first.

"We've set up the radio over there," Fishman went on, "and

Wood will stay to liaise with Dr. Zelenka."

The corporal looked up, hearing her name, and then bent back over her wires and boxes.

"We were going to leave a naquadah generator, but Dr. Kasper says they may be able to get power turned on in the plant itself," Fishman said. "The docs back on Atlantis were complaining that they didn't have a lot of spare generators right now."

"Ok," Lorne said, and the double doors at the back of the hall swung open.

"There you are," Kasper said. "Dr. Zelenka wanted me to warn you that we are about to start the internal generator."

"Ok," Lorne said, sounding wary, and Wood looked up again.

"That's good, right, sir?"

"How long have you been on Atlantis?" Fishman asked, and she frowned, looking suddenly very young.

"About three months —"

There was a deep rumble, more felt than heard, and the overhead lights flickered. Ronon looked up, checking for missing bulbs, and they flickered again, then steadied to a dull orange glow that brightened rapidly.

"Excellent!" Kasper exclaimed, and darted back through the double doors.

Ronon looked at Lorne, seeing his own uncertainty reflected in the major's face. "Better check for short circuits."

"Yeah." Lorne nodded to Fishman, and they made a quick circuit of the lobby. Somewhat to Ronon's surprise, there were no broken wires spitting sparks, no smoke curling from between panels, just the line of chandeliers glowing in the center of the open room. It had been years since he'd seen anything like it, Ronon realized — Atlantis's lights were different, and the lights on Earth had been a subtly different color — and he allowed himself a moment just to stare.

The double doors swung open again, and the engineers emerged, looking and sounding pleased with themselves.

"See, everything's working —"

"Beautiful!"

"I told you that was the procedure," Kos said, to Pin, and he nodded.

"And you were right, absolutely right."

Zelenka detached himself from the group and came to join them. "We are making progress. If the other generators are in as good shape, there is no reason we can't get them working again as well."

"That's great news," Lorne said. "But now I should get my people back to Atlantis."

"Actually," Zelenka said, "I was hoping you would stay overnight, just in case we had any problems with the systems here."

"You're not seriously suggesting we might need to evacuate everybody," Lorne said.

"No, no." Zelenka shook his head. "I was thinking that if we had more confidence in the station's system, we could send the naquadah generator back with you. There are backup batteries for the radio if we need them, yes? And it's not as though we have so many naquadah generators to spare."

"True enough." Lorne paused. "Let me radio Atlantis, see what the colonel says."

He moved away, and Ronon looked up at the blazing chandeliers. Just seeing them felt like a celebration. "Do you think we can get the plant working again? Send power to the capital?"

"Ah." Zelenka gave a wry smile. "Those are two very different things. The people here, they did an excellent job of mothballing the plant. It is all almost ready to start up tomorrow. But to get power to the capital — you saw how many transmission lines were lost. That is a project on an entirely different scale."

"Still." It was impossible to be a pessimist standing there in the brightly-lit lobby while the sun went down outside. "We need the wires, right, the cables? And we need to string them. The towers look like they're in good shape —"

"The ones we've seen," Zelenka said. "And neither the road nor the railroad seems to be in good repair."

"We'll find a way," Ronon said. "We can bring some of it up by puddle jumper, or in the Rapide — Lorne thinks there's room to land here. And we can take carts along the road." He faltered, reality setting in. That was years of work, salvaging the cable, hauling it through the woods; repairing the road would take nearly as long, and the railroad even longer, if they could even find people who knew how to do the work, because Atlantis wouldn't — couldn't — provide that much help...

"I think it's worth doing," Zelenka said, and Ronon gave him a startled look. "But it will be better if no one expects it to be easy. Or fast. But I think it will get done in the end."

"Yeah," Ronon said, and thought he did believe it. Zelenka gave him a quick smile, and turned away.

"Excuse me."

Ronon turned to see Valiena Bar looking up at him. She had obviously been helping out in the generator room, her hands and pullover stained with rust and darker grime, and there was a streak of oil on her chin. "Yeah?"

"If Major Lorne is flying back tonight — he won't be able to see anyone on the ground."

Her brother had been with Evrast Mar, Ronon remembered. "I thought they were going up the other side of the Spur."

"They were going to the Spur," Bar said. "Atil said last time they took the road part of the way because it was easier than cutting cross country. I thought the Lanteans said they would look for him."

"Lorne's probably not going back until tomorrow morning," Ronon said. "I'll talk to him."

"Thank you."

Ronon frowned. "Is there any particular reason you're worried? Anything we ought to know about?"

"I'm worried because they didn't check in," Bar answered. "Anything could happen up here."

That was true — and it was exactly why Cai tried to keep the number of exploring missions to a minimum of people who knew what they were doing — but there was something about the question that made him frown. Was she more worried than he would have expected? She had to have known the risks. He shook the thought away. There was enough to do to get the power plant secured for the night; he'd worry about her in the morning.

***

Mel let the video play through to its end again, this time watching Cai as he studied the images. Lorne had done a good job surveying what was left of the roadway as well as the surrounding terrain; it was just a matter now of convincing Sateda's governor that it was time to put the Rapide to the test. He knew it, she thought, but just hated making that last leap. Lorne had made it back to the capital a little after noon, and hung around to answer questions before taking the puddle jumper back to Atlantis. From everything he'd said, it sounded as though the scientists expected to be able to get the plant running again, and she hoped that news would put Cai in a better mood.

"You're sure you can land there?" Cai said, and turned the laptop back to face her. "The paving isn't in very good shape. And you're sure there's enough room?"

"Major Lorne estimates that we have about two thousand yards from the southern end of the clearing to the plant perimeter," Mel answered. "That's comfortably more than the minimum. Ronon's already started clearing those little trees. And, of course, we're not actually planning to need to land there."

Cai smiled at that, the oil lamps flickering. "All right. If we agree that this is an acceptable emergency landing zone — then what? What exactly are you trying to achieve?"

Mel reached for the map she had brought from the field. It was the best they had, a copy of a copy of a real survey-style map, traced onto brittle sheets salvaged from an office supply house, and she unfolded it carefully. It showed the edge of the Alduren Plateau and the Spur trailing south and east off its edge, a knife's edge of rock rising from the forest. The Narmoth Falls and the power plant were on the western side, at the western edge of the map; the eastern slope of the Spur was marked with squares and crosses and tiny names. "The Spur is on the edge of our planned survey area — we'd have taken in more of it, but it's at the farthest extent of our range, and we've had problems with turbulence, since there's a fairly stiff downslope wind on the eastern side of the mountains. After we got those first pictures, though, we tried a second run, and got some more images that suggest that there's a man-made clearing here —" She touched the map beside a square that lay just below the edge of the Plateau, high on the slopes of the Spur. "We think it might be in current use."

Cai squinted at the map. "That's the old Wild Blue mine."

"Yes?" Mel still didn't read Satedan very well.

"A silver mine, I think," Cai said. "It was mostly silver and lead up there."

"That would make sense." Mel touched keys, calling up the drone photographs. "We've done our best to enhance these, but they're not very clear. This one, though… That's the same area we saw before, and it's definitely cut timber."

Cai nodded. "Could have been from before the attack, though."

"I agree." Mel called up the next image. "But this — it isn't as clear, but it looks as though that's a trail there. Yustyna — Yustyna Tan, she's been doing most of the enhancement and analysis — she says that the bushes would have grown back if it wasn't in recent use. And this one could be the roof of a building."

"There were plenty of buildings up there around the mines," Cai said. "Little towns, the mine buildings themselves. That trail, though…"

Mel bit her tongue to keep from talking, watching him page forward and back through the file of pictures. She had learned long ago that it was better not to oversell her ideas; she'd made the best case she could, and now it was up to Cai. And they both knew it was time to give the Rapide a proper test.

"All right." Cai slid the laptop back to her again. "If I say yes, what's your plan?"

Mel was careful not to smile. "It looks as though we've got a stretch of good weather coming up, so my idea is to take Yustyna as photographer and fly up the west side of the Spur."

"The west side?"

"That way we wouldn't have to cross the Spur until we were sure everything was working properly, and we'd be right in line for Narmoth Falls if we had any problems. Plus we could follow the rail line north, and wouldn't have to worry about navigating. Once we reach the Falls, turn east, cross the Spur, and fly a search pattern over the likely area." She circled the northern end of the Spur, centered on the mine Cai had named the Wild Blue. "We'll have time to cover it thoroughly and still make it back to the field before sundown."

Cai rubbed his chin, then nodded. "All right. When do you want to go?"

"Tomorrow." Mel spread her hands. "We're ready, and the weather is ideal. There's no point in delaying."

"All right," Cai said again. "Confirm with Dex that the landing strip is clear, and — you have permission."

***

Mel made her way to the airfield in the rising light, a thermos of Earth coffee in her hand to mark the occasion. The radio operator at the power plant had confirmed that the landing strip was clear, though Wood warned that the surface was still rough enough to damage tires. If we end up landing there, that'll be the least of our worries, Mel thought. The Rapide was already pushed out onto the well-mown grass, both Satedan and Air Force technicians making their final checks. Tan broke away from the others and came to meet her, heavy camera bouncing against her chest.

"Are we going?"

Mel nodded. "Everything's in order. The governor sends his best wishes."

Tan broke into an excited grin. "We're ready. We've been ready."

"I know," Mel said. "But now — now we go."

Emergency supplies were tucked into the rear of the cabin, and Mel checked them quickly, making sure that everything was there and balanced for takeoff. They had supplies to last ten days if they were forced down, and that was plenty of time for someone from Atlantis to collect them in a puddle jumper. If they survived, of course, a voice whispered at the back of her mind, but she pushed that aside. The Rapide was one of the sturdiest kit-built planes available, and she and McKay and the rest of Atlantis's crew had modified the frame to make it even stronger. If she had to set down in the woods, she was pretty sure the Rapide would hold together. That didn't mean the engines couldn't blow up — she still didn't really understand how McKay had managed to adapt the naquadah generator to power the Rapide's propellers — but that was another thing she wasn't going to think about. Everything had worked fine in the tests, and there was no reason to think things would be any different just because she was going to be a few hundred miles further from the capital.

She did her walk-around, checking the exterior for any problems, any systems that were out of adjustment or anything that they might have forgotten. As usual, the Rapide was clean, the sleek white hull gleaming in the sun, and she ducked under the wing and out around the canard that jutted from the nose. That was one of the things that made the Rapide so suited for this job, keeping it stable even in the turbulence that came off the mountains; between that and the twin engines in the rear, she doubted she'd need to worry too much about the downslope winds on the eastern side of the Spur. It was just a pity they didn't have a satellite in orbit to read the weather for her, but she could manage.

Tan climbed past her into the cabin, and she heard the camera hatch in the Rapide's belly slide open. A moment later, the boxy lens poked below the hull, and the latches clicked into place.

"Everything in order?" the chief mechanic called from the hangar door, and Mel waved in answer.

"It all looks good! Ready to start engines."

"Go ahead," the mechanic answered, and Mel hauled herself into the cabin, then pulled the door closed behind her. She dogged it shut and stepped over Tan, who was lying on the deck making final adjustments to the camera, to settle herself in the pilot's seat.

"I'm ready to start the engines," she called, and a moment later Tan scrambled forward to take the co-pilot's seat.

"Shall I handle the radio?" Tan's voice was calm, as though she'd been flying all her life, not taken her first ride less than three months ago.

"Please." At least there were no complicated traffic control proceedings to worry about, Mel thought, as she got the engines running and waited for them to warm up. This must have been what it was like in the last century back on Earth, back when aviation was just getting started. You got in your plane, fired up the engines, and took off whenever you pleased. "Tell everyone I'm ready to taxi," she said aloud, and heard Tan relay the information.

"The landing strip's clear."

"All right." Mel eased the throttle forward, the Rapide jolting forward over the close-cut grass, then turned into the light wind. "Ready for take-off."

"You're cleared," the chief mechanic answered, the voice crackling in her headphones. "Good luck and safe journey."

"Thanks." Mel checked rudder and elevators one last time, and advanced the throttle. In the same moment, she released the brakes and the Rapide leaped forward, engines roaring. The nose came up quickly, and she tugged the control column back, feeling the wings catch the air. The Rapide rose, easily clearing the wrecked buildings at the end of the strip, and she watched the instruments as the city dropped away beneath them. She circled once at 500 feet, a lazy left-hand turn to make sure everything felt right, then checked her compass and settled onto the heading that would take them toward the railroad line. The sky was clear except for a few wisps of cloud far above them — fifteen thousand feet, she guessed, and she wasn't taking the Rapide anywhere near them.

"It's a beautiful day for flying," she said aloud, and saw Tan grin in answer.

***

Ronon surveyed the cleared length of roadway with satisfaction, stretching a little to work the kinks out of his back and neck. They had gotten all the saplings cut and cleared the day before; most of the wood was cut and trimmed and stacked to season, and the smallest bits were piled at each end of the runway to make bonfires if the Rapide needed to land after dark. That would be a real emergency, of course, and if the Rapide was forced to make the attempt by firelight, the condition of the runway would be the least of Hocken's worries.

He put that thought aside, turning slowly to survey the clearing. Bar and a Satedan technician named Tec were finishing the last sweep of the pavement, pushing brooms that Kos had found in one of the supply closets. They were coming steadily closer, leaving little puffs of dust in their wake, and Ronon thought the landing strip was about as ready as it was going to be. On the other side of the clearing, the windows of the power plant glowed even in the daylight, and the sound of the turbines blended with the roar of the falls. The generator was still functioning perfectly, and the engineers had professed themselves certain of being able to start the rest of the generators once there was somewhere to send the power. Of course, that meant restringing what seemed like an impossible length of power line, but the scientists were treating it as though it were in fact possible. And if it could be done, there would be enough power in the capital to lure more Satedans back to their world. It might even be possible to get some of the factories running again.

Tec lifted a hand in greeting as the pair reached the end of the pavement. "Any word from the capital?"

"Not yet —" He broke off as his radio clicked on.

"Sir, I have Colonel Hocken on air," Wood said, from the radio station inside the plant's lobby. "She thinks she's about twenty minutes out, and wants to know if the landing strip is ready."

"Can you put me through?" Ronon looked up again, though the Rapide would be too far out to see.

"Patching you through."

Static crackled, and Hocken said, "Ronon, do you copy?"

"I hear you," Ronon answered. "The landing strip is as good as it's going to get."

"Could you be a bit more specific?"

"All the little trees are cut down and we've cleared all debris." Ronon paused. "You might want to take a look before you decide if it's good enough for an emergency."

"I figured that would be a good plan." Ronon could hear momentary laughter in Hocken's voice, and then she sobered. "I'll circle over the area and take a good look, and if everything seems in order, I'll make a low-altitude pass to check it out. That all right with you?"

He was, Ronon realized abruptly, the senior officer at the power plant, by either Satedan or Lantean reckoning. "Yeah, go ahead."

"Copy that," Hocken said. "We're coming up from the south, following the road."

"We'll be looking for you." Out of the corner of his eye, Ronon could see the rest of the team spilling out of the plant, peering up into the sky and pointing.

"Here," Tec said, to Bar, "I'll take that in for you."

Bar smiled her thanks, and Tec balanced both brooms on his shoulder, heading toward the plant. Bar looked back at Ronon. "Did — I don't suppose they've seen anything?"

"Hocken?"

Bar nodded. "I know they weren't really looking, but maybe —"

"She didn't say anything. I'll ask once she's made her fly-over." Ronon paused. "You're really worried about your brother."

She gave a little shrug. "Well, of course. They were supposed to check in, and we haven't heard anything."

"I thought he was used to going into the back country."

"He's done it before," Bar answered. "And General Mar is very good."

"Yeah. So I've heard." The radio buzzed again, and he looked up to see a tiny dot moving toward them just above the treetops.

"Ronon," Hocken said. "I've got the clearing and the plant in site — is it just me, or are things in good shape down there?"

"They're not bad," Ronon answered. "How's the Rapide?"

"Flies like a dream," Hocken answered, and there was no mistaking the satisfaction in her voice. "You can tell Dr. McKay that the generator works like a charm."

"Copy that." Ronon watched as the Rapide came closer, changing from a dot to a dot with wings to the familiar shape. He could hear the engines now, loud enough to be heard even over the sound of the falls, and thought that any survivors would at least respond to the noise.

The Rapide tipped into a lazy turn, pivoting on the downward wingtip, swung back over the clearing. "Everything looks good," Hocken said. "I'm going to make a pass over the strip, and if that looks good, I'll do another at treetop level. Wood, what's the wind speed?"

"Five knots from the north northeast," Wood answered promptly. "Downdraft off the Plateau."

"Five knots from the north-northeast," Hocken repeated. "Copy that."

Ronon shaded his eyes as the Rapide circled back toward them, shedding altitude. Hocken steered the Rapide the length of the landing strip, then pulled up again, banking west to circle back to the southern end of the field.

"Looks good. I'm coming in at treetop level."

"Go ahead," Ronon answered.

The Rapide turned again, dropping more rapidly this time, until its wheels seemed about to brush the tops of the trees. Once past the clearing's edge, it dropped even lower, the short-winged nose coming up, and it roared the full length of the cleared strip before Hocken pulled it up and away.

"I can land there," she said. "It looks great."

That filled Cai's requirement, and Ronon nodded. "Ok. Then you're cleared to check out the drone sightings. Question before you go, Colonel."

"Go ahead."

"A group went out into the back country and hasn't checked in. Did you see any sign that they'd been through?"

"Negative," Hocken answered, the Rapide spiraling up and away from the clearing. "We weren't looking, though, and all that country's pretty heavily wooded."

"Understood, thanks," Ronon said.

"Ask her if she could see any damaged transmission towers," Zelenka said abruptly.

Ronon hadn't seen him approach, but keyed the radio. "One more question. Could you see any damaged transmission towers?"

"That's a negative, too," Hocken answered. "We could see some intact, but the road was heavily overgrown in spots. Yustyna has good video, though."

"See if you can get another look on the way back," Ronon said. "If it doesn't affect the mission."

"Roger that," Hocken answered. "We'll be in touch once we start the search pattern."

"Copy that, Colonel," Wood answered. "Good luck."

"Thanks," Hocken answered, and the Rapide turned again, rising over the edge of the Plateau.

"Anything?" Zelenka asked, and Ronon shook his head.

"She had video, we'll have to wait until it's downloaded."

Zelenka sighed. "I suppose I didn't expect any better. Still, if we could just get those power lines back up —"

"We'd be in good shape," Ronon said.

CHAPTER THREE

MEL LET the Rapide climb to three thousand feet as they crossed the edge of the Plateau. Below the Rapide's wing, the Tellhart River wound through a landscape of grass and scrubby trees, to vanish abruptly over the plateau's edge. There had been ruins at the top of the falls, a roofless stone shell of a building, and she remembered that the Eze family had said there was a switchback path from there down to the power plant. Presumably both had originally been part of the power system, though she hadn't thought to ask before they left. Not that it really mattered, either, and she glanced again at her controls. All the instruments were in perfect order, and she checked the compass heading, then tipped the Rapide into a shallow turn. The world wheeled beneath her, the Rapide beautifully responsive to the slightest touch, and she saw Tan crane her head to see out the side window.

"Spot anything?"

Tan shook her head as the Rapide leveled out again. "Just the top of the falls. Did I see that they had the power working in the plant?"

"I didn't notice," Mel confessed.

"I suppose you were thinking of other things," Tan conceded. "It's good to have another place to land."

"Yeah. With luck, it'll persuade the governor to let us push a little further north."

"Maybe we could even bring some of the drones to the Falls, set up another base. We could still use the transmitter at Escavera as a beacon."

"That's a possibility," Mel said, but her attention was on

her instruments. No satellites orbited Sateda, there was no GPS to guide her, only the radio stations at the capital and Narmoth Falls and Escavera for relative bearings, and the local compass to give her a heading. She was glad she'd kept current in civilian planes and ultralights: this was like the early days of aviation, before radar and direction-finding radios; she was glad to have a good view of the ground, and solid landmarks to steer by.

She checked her position against the line of the Spur, the steep treeless ridge sharp as a knife's blade before the dark rock gave way to easier slopes and scrubby conifers. Supposedly there were a dozen mines cut into this side of the Spur, where the slopes were shallower and the ore more accessible, though some of them had been closed before the Wraith came. That didn't mean that someone couldn't be living in the shelter of a played-out mine, so they'd need to make a couple of passes to be sure they covered all of them. She glanced at the space where the fuel indicator had been, and instead saw the bars that showed output from the pocket naquadah generator glowing green, quivering at the line that indicated seventy percent of maximum power. That had proved to be their most efficient range in the trials, and she was pleased to see it holding true on this flight.

"I'm going back to set up the still cameras," Tan said, unbuckling her harness, and Mel nodded.

"Ok. Let me know when you're ready."

"Will do."

Mel swung the Rapide north again, looking for the break a few miles south of where the Spur met the Plateau. Supposedly there was a mine just below that point, on the eastern slope; if she could spot that, she could get a decent compass heading to follow for her search pattern.

"Camera's in place," Tan said, over the intercom. "Video's

still running if you want it."

"Copy that." Mel flipped the switch that engaged the small screen set between the pilots' consoles, and the image of the terrain beneath them swam into focus. "Ok. I've got the notch in sight. I'm going to swing back north and drop down to five hundred feet for the pass."

"Careful of the wind," Tan said.

"Copy that." Mel tightened her hold on the steering column as she spoke. On this side of the Spur, everyone reported strong downslope winds, and sure enough as she dropped through six hundred feet the Rapide jerked and shuddered. She brought it back onto its line, feeling the turbulence bouncing her like an old car on a country road. "Can you get pictures in this?"

"I'll try…"

"I can try at seven hundred, we might get above it."

"Maybe — wait."

There was a note in Tan's voice that brought Mel to full alertness, though her hands didn't move on the controls. "You all right?"

"Yes, fine. We've got to go back, I think — I'm sure there was something there."

Mel risked a glance at the video screen, but it showed nothing but the tops of more trees. She tipped the Rapide into a shallow, careful turn, working with the wind, and steadied onto a reciprocal course. The Rapide bounced, swaying from side to side, and she focused on her instruments, trying to keep the plane level.

"There!"

Mel risked a quick glance at the video screen, but saw only a break in the eternal trees before she had to turn her attention back to the controls. "What have you got?"

"That clearing — somebody's been using it."

"Recently?" As soon as she said the word, Mel realized it was a stupid question. "Sorry. Coming around again."

"Can you get any lower?"

"I'll try." Mel banked the Rapide, pressing the nose down, and leveled out again at four hundred feet. The air was a little steadier here, and she let the airspeed drop. A light flickered for a moment on the instrument, and she frowned: the port engine was running a little hot. She touched the generator control, reducing power to the port engine, and saw the light go out, the numbers falling back to normal. "Four hundred feet."

"Coming up…"

Mel glanced at the screen again, and this time she saw it, too, the edges of a clearing too regular to be natural, water flowing in raised wooden sluices, a stack of timber too neat to be anything but recent. "How close are we to the mine head?"

"Not sure," Tan answered. "A couple of miles downslope? Can you give me another pass? I want to get some more pictures?"

"Copy that," Mel answered, checking the terrain. There was room enough, and she turned the Rapide toward the Spur. "I'm going to see if I can spot the mine, see if that's where they're living."

"Ok. I'll try for pictures."

Mel checked her airspeed again. The Rapide was designed to handle low speeds without stalling, but the rough air made it hard to hold the plane steady. She glanced quickly out the side window, seeing the steep rise of the Spur seemingly only a few yards from her wingtip, a sharp line where the trees gave way to scree and rock. Yes, there was the mine, a black opening in the mountainside, the clearing in front of it trampled mud, bare of grass and timber. The handful of buildings looked empty, the windows broken out and doors hanging from their hinges, but the timber sluice ran all the way to the entrance, and it looked as though the trees had been cut back recently.

"Got it," Tan called. "Video and still."

A sudden gust shook the Rapide, and Mel pulled the nose up. "Copy. One more pass over the clearing?"

"If you can," Tan answered, and Mel checked her instruments. The port engine was still running hotter than its twin, but it was within the limits.

"One more at four hundred. I'll try for three, but the wind's getting tougher."

"Four hundred's fine."

"Four hundred, then."

Mel brought the Rapide around again, lining up for the next pass. "I'm going to radio Narmoth Falls, let them know what we've got."

"Go ahead," Tan answered, and Mel flicked the radio selector.

"Narmoth Falls, this is Rapide. Do you copy? Narmoth Falls, this is Rapide."

The answer was reassuringly prompt, Wood's voice clear despite the mountains between them. "Rapide, Narmoth Falls. We copy. Everything all right?"

"We see signs of current habitation at the first mine site below the notch," Mel said. "I don't know the name of the mine, but it looks like someone's living there, or trying to get it working, or both."

"Copy that," Wood said. "Hey, that's good news, right?"

"Should be." Mel checked the port engine again. "Pass that on to Ronon, please."

"Roger that," Wood answered. "Are you going to proceed with the rest of the search?"

"Yes, unless we spot people on the ground. I'll let you know if anything changes. Rapide out." Mel flicked the selector back to the intercom. "How are you doing?"

"One more pass?"

Mel grinned — she had never yet flown reconnaissance without being asked for "just one more" — and a red light flashed among her controls. The port engine temperature spiked again, shooting past the normal limits to pin the indicator against the top of the column. Mel swore under her breath, turning the dial to reduce power again. The indicator dropped a little, but it was still into the red zone. "Negative," she said aloud. "We've got a problem."

"Do you need me up front?" Tan's voice was unnaturally controlled.

"Negative." Mel adjusted the generator's output, bringing the port engine's temperature down a little further. It seemed to stabilize a little, and she pulled back on the yoke, lifting the Rapide toward the thirteen hundred feet she would need to clear the Plateau. Another light flashed, warning that the engine wasn't getting enough power; she adjusted the feed again, and watched the temperature climb. "Damn it. Yustyna, better get up here after all, I think we're losing an engine."

She fiddled with the power control, trying to keep the engine running, but the temperature continued to climb. Tan slid into the co-pilot's seat, fastening the harness across her body, and said, "Do you want me to radio Narmoth Falls?"

"Not yet," Mel began, and the Rapide shuddered as she let the power drop again. "Damn it! I'm going to have to shut down the port engine."

"How bad is that?"

"We can fly on one, that's no problem — that's why we bought the twin-engine." Mel flicked switches, running through the shutdown procedure. The port engine sputtered and died, and she feathered the propeller to reduce drag. The starboard engine whined up in answer, and she eyed the temperature gauge warily. "Yeah, call the Falls, tell them we're coming back to them. We should be able to set down there, see what's gone wrong —"

She broke off as the Rapide tried to fall off to the right, caught in a sudden gust of wind. She brought it back, and heard Tan speaking into the microphone, her voice still tight.

"Narmoth Falls, this is Rapide. We have an engine problem."

Mel closed her mind to the conversation, concentrating on the feel of the controls and the instrument displays. The Rapide was harder to control with only one engine, and she had to apply nearly full rudder to balance the uneven power; the nose canard damped the tendency to stall and spin, but it was hard to keep it steady. She increased power, boosting the Rapide toward the edge of the Plateau. She'd clear it now by about a hundred feet, but she wanted more room.

"Mel. Narmoth Falls says you're free to land any time, and to keep them informed."

"Ok." Mel pulled the yoke back again. A little more lift, just a little more, or she'd need to circle back away from the Plateau, and she didn't want to waste the time. The Rapide rose, the controls sluggish in her hands. A hundred and fifty feet of clearance, almost two hundred —

A light flashed on the starboard engine's monitor, and a tone sounded: the starboard engine was overheating, too. Mel swore and reached across to reduce power as much as she dared. The engine faltered, but the temperature didn't drop. They were almost at the Plateau, almost above its edge. Mel's breath caught in her throat as she saw the rock rising in front of them, and she eased the throttle forward just a hair. For a moment, nothing happened, but then the Rapide rose, clearing the cliff's edge by about a hundred feet.

That was only one problem solved. The overheating warning sounded again, and Mel craned her neck to see out the windscreen and side windows. On this side of the Tellhart, the ground was open, a flat grassy meadow stretching a good mile or more to the trees. That was a bit of luck, and Mel adjusted the flaps, lining the Rapide up so that the cliff would be off the starboard wing and she would have the longest open stretch available before they reached the trees.

"We're losing the starboard engine, too. I'm going to have to set us down."

"Ok," Tan said, and Mel heard her repeat the message to Narmoth Falls.

Mel checked the trim again. There wasn't time for finesse, not if she wanted to make the landing while the starboard engine was still running, but she'd already lost a lot of speed and altitude. She pulled the nose up just a hair, concentrating on the grass unreeling under her nose. As long as it was as clear as it looked… It would be or it wouldn't. She let the Rapide stall, and dropped it neatly onto the meadow.

The Rapide bounced and settled, jolting toward the trees. Mel worked the controls, not daring to brake too hard on the uneven ground, and at last the Rapide slowed and stopped. The starboard engine was still showing dangerous heat, and she shut it down quickly, then for good measure took the naquaddah generator into stand-by mode, leaving just enough power to run the electrical systems. Everything was suddenly very quiet, just the ticking of cooling metal, and then Tan gave a shaky laugh.

"Well. I guess we can say the plane will land on open ground."

"Yeah." Mel loosened her harness. "Radio Narmoth Falls and tell them we're all right. I'm going to take a look at the engines."

"Will do," Tan said, and Mel hauled herself out of the pilot's seat. She'd made emergency landings before, some of them in conditions that were objectively a lot more dangerous, but as she opened the hatch and let down the cabin stairs, she was painfully aware of how far they were from help. Even under the best possible conditions, it would take several hours for a puddle jumper to reach them from Atlantis; if they had gone down without time to radio their position or warn Narmoth Falls, it could take days or even weeks for a puddle jumper to find them. And if they couldn't rely on Atlantis's help — She shook herself. She had known what she was getting into when she took the job. No matter how much she told herself this was just like working in Antarctica or someplace like that, the fact remained that this was an alien planet in another galaxy. She was a very long way from home.

***

Radek let out a sigh of relief as Tan's voice crackled through the speaker.

"We're down safely, no damage to the aircraft — except whatever was already wrong with it, of course."

"Copy that," Wood said, the relief everyone was feeling audible in her voice. "Can you give us your location?"

"Yes." There was a pause, and a scrabbling sound, as though Tan was moving papers in the cockpit. "We're on the edge of the Plateau, on the eastern side of the Tellhart, maybe four or five miles from the bank? It's grid square A25 on our map. The edge of the plateau is maybe a mile of open meadow before you get to the trees."

Ronon reached for a microphone. Most of the crew had gathered in the lobby as soon as words had circulated that the Rapide was in trouble; probably most of them ought to get back to work, Radek thought, but doubted anyone was going to move.

"What went wrong with the engine?"

"It overheated?" Tan paused. "Mel's out looking at the engines now —"

"Narmoth Falls, this is Hocken. Sorry to interrupt, but I can give you some data directly now."

"Go ahead," Ronon said, and Radek reached for his tablet, ready to make notes. He hadn't worked on the Rapide himself, but he was familiar with what Rodney had done to make the pocket generator viable.

"The first indication of a problem was an overheat warning on the port engine," Hocken said. "I decreased power from the generator, and that helped for a little, but it kept getting worse. I shut down the port engine, figuring we'd make it back to the Falls on the other, and the same thing happened with it."

Radek looked over the top of his glasses. "Colonel, this is Zelenka. Did the starboard engine overheat at the same rate as the port?"

There was a little pause. "Faster, I think."

"Ok. Go on."

Ronon gave him a look, but Hocken took him at his word. "I've got the cowlings opened up now," she finished, "and I'm not seeing any signs of damage in the engine itself. Looks like I got it shut down in time. The problem is, I'm also not seeing anything that looks like it could have caused the problem."

"The oil is full, then," Radek said, "and all the coolants."

"Confirmed."

Radek flipped pages on the tablet, scrolling through the Rapide's schematics. "No signs of fire?"

"Nothing."

"No changes in oil pressure before the warning?"

"No." Hocken paused. "We were flying low and slow, so I was looking for exactly that problem. But these engines have secondary cooling, it's not just airflow."

"Yes." Radek frowned at the tablet. "What about the generator itself?"

"I haven't touched it," Hocken said, sounding faintly defensive.

The naquaddah generators were meant to be sealed boxes; most Atlantis personnel were taught that they were to be handled by trained personnel only. "Did it give any warnings?" Radek asked.

"Oh. No, nothing. Power output was completely normal."

"Can you open its containment, please? Just to see?"

"Yeah. Give me a minute."

Radek flicked through the checklists again, frowning, then looked up to see Ronon looking down at him.

"Is that something she can fix?"

"The generator?" Radek shook his head. "No, probably not. But I don't think that's the problem. Rodney set up a very good set of sensors, if there was anything wrong, it should have told her so." Unless it was a kind of failure they hadn't encountered before, and therefore didn't know to warn about.

"Whoa!" Hocken's voice came sharply through the speakers, and everyone jumped.

Ronon said, "You all right, Hocken?"

"Yeah, I'm fine, but I think I've found the problem."

"The generator?" Radek's heart sank. That would mean days of repair work, readying a replacement generator, and before that they'd have to find out what had actually gone wrong —

"Not the generator," Hocken answered. "It's the connection between the generator and the engines. I opened up the generator, and I could feel the heat coming off this conduit."

"Is the conduit actually damaged?" Radek demanded. That was better than he'd hoped — as long as the conduit still worked, Hocken could get the Rapide back to the Falls and he could make more permanent repairs here. "Tell me what you see."

"Hang on, I've got to get a flashlight —" The radio carried some indistinct scuffling, and then Hocken said, more clearly, "Ok, I can see — it looks like all the lines are intact, and I don't see any scorching, either on the wires or on the composite around them. But it's still hot in there."

Radek scrolled back through the schematics until he found the section that covered the connections. There was less insulation than he would have expected, given the amount of power that the lines would have to carry, and he shook his head. "Ok. And you said you were flying low, with high power output?"

"That's right."

"So, yes, that puts some strain on the transfer." Radek found the diagram he was looking for, frowned at the screen. "Ok. There are a couple of possibilities here, but everything has to wait for the conduit to cool completely. I will call you back once I have options for you."

"Ok, Dr. Zelenka," Hocken said.

"Check in every hour," Ronon said. "Counting from now."

"Will do," Hocken said, and the transmission ended.

Radek set the tablet on the nearest console. According to the schematic, the area around the conduit was supposed to be insulated; that was the first thing he needed to check, to see if that had actually been done, though from what Hocken had said he suspected it had not. But if there was an engine overheat indicator, then that wasn't the only problem, and his next guess would be that the step-down transformer McKay had placed to modulate the generator's output wasn't up to the job. That would explain both the heat in the conduit and the engine itself overheating. That was easily enough fixed, but not with the parts he had at hand. He became aware that

Ronon was staring at him, and lifted his head. "Yes?"

"Can you fix this?"

"Probably." Radek glanced at the screen again. "I think that once the conduit cools down they will be able to take off and fly here without encountering any more problems. Possibly they could get as far as the capital, since they reached us without problems, but I think that would be taking an unnecessary risk. It would also be possible to drill some small holes here in the engine nacelle to improve cooling, but I would prefer not to do that unless we have to."

"So you want her to fly back here." Ronon sounded doubtful.

"Yes." Radek turned the tablet so that he could see the plans. "Look, I think the problem is here, with this transformer. It needs to be able to handle higher loads than originally calculated — we did not take into account what would happen with low speed but high reserve power."

"We don't have any of those transformers, do we?" Ronon asked.

Radek cocked his head in question. "Do you mean here, or at all?"

"Both."

"No. Also to both. McKay will have to build some." Radek sighed. "I suppose I will have to tell him so."

"He's all yours," Ronon said.

***

Mel left the cowlings open to let the slight breeze pass through the engines and the compartment that held the connecting conduit, then made a quick circuit of the Rapide, checking for any other damage. Everything else seemed fine, even the tires, despite the grass caught in the landing gear, and she rounded the nose, ducking under the canard, to see Tan sitting on the top of the cabin steps, a Satedan water bottle in her hand. She held it out as Mel approached, and Mel took it with a nod of thanks, downing a mouthful of lukewarm tea.

"Anything new from the Falls?" She handed the bottle back, and Tan drank in turn.

"Not yet. I checked in a while ago and they're still trying to decide what we ought to do."

"Right." There was room on the steps for two, and Mel settled herself one step below the other woman, looking around the clearing. The Plateau was astonishingly beautiful, even by the Satedan standards. The knee-high grass stretched lush and green all the way to the bank of the Tellhart, marked by a scattering of low trees that rattled round green-gold leaves in the wind. A cloud of spray rose like fog from the falls, a rainbow poised in its heart where the setting sun caught it, and beyond the edge of the cliff, the purple-brown rock of the Spur stretched south and east, the darker green of the conifers rising along its flanks. "Did they have any suggestions?"

Tan breathed a laugh. "It sounds as though Dr. Zelenka and Dr. McKay are fighting that out right now. Are they always like this?"

"Pretty much," Mel said. And that was something she wasn't going to miss, not like she missed electricity and indoor plumbing.

"Do you think they're going to come up with an answer?"

"Oh, yeah." Mel accepted the thermos again, and took a long drink. "In fact, I think we could probably fly out of here once everything is thoroughly cooled down — we could land back at the Falls, and then Dr. Zelenka could take a look at things instead of having to guess."

"I'd like that better than sleeping in the airplane," Tan said, with a grin, and Mel pushed herself to her feet.

"Me, too. I'm going to check the conduits. If they've cooled down, I'll radio the Falls and tell them I want to fly back."

"Ok."

Mel handed back the thermos, and ducked under the wing to check the conduit. It was a lot cooler than it had been, just warm to the touch, and she glanced back at the sun. There were still several more hours of flying time left before she'd have to worry about losing the light, even considering that she was going to be dropping down below the Plateau's edge. Still, it was probably a good idea to check in with the Falls and make sure she wasn't missing anything important.

She heard a thud from the front of the plane, and then a scuffling noise. She froze, wishing she was carrying her service pistol, but it was back in the cabin — the plain had been utterly empty, though she should have considered that there might be wild animals. But Tan would have said if that was likely —

She was moving in the same instant, fading back between the engines, stooped to duck beneath the Rapide's belly. She could see boots, more than one pair of them, and then Tan's feet, stepping away from the stairs. Mel swallowed a curse, furious at herself, at her own carelessness, and heard Tan's voice sharp with fear.

"Who are you? What do you want?"

"That's our question," a man answered. "You — I see you under there. Come out, or I'll shoot your friend."

Mel swore again, but there was no place to run. She heard the snap as someone cocked an old-fashioned bolt rifle, and slid hastily out from between the engines. "Don't shoot! I'm coming."

She came wide around the tip of the wing, her hands in the air, to see a group of four men — no, she amended, seeing several more standing well back, there were at least eight of them, and they'd placed themselves so that they could easily cover the area around the plane. They had to have come from the woods, she thought, then snuck up using the plane itself as cover. Probably they had been lying flat in the grass when she made her last walk-around, and it hadn't occurred to her to look. That was the sort of carelessness that would have gotten her killed back in the Milky Way — would have gotten her killed on any number of Earthside deployments — and she wanted to kick herself. She'd gotten too comfortable on Sateda.

"What's the problem?" she asked, and the oldest of the men turned, covering her with his rifle. "We don't want any trouble —"

"Shut up," one of the other men snapped. He looked young and scared, and Mel spread her hands carefully, showing both palms empty. He was the immediate danger, and she did her best to look unthreatening.

"Who are you?" That was the oldest man. "And what is this — thing?" He jerked his head at the Rapide.

Mel kept her face expressionless with an effort. When they'd chosen the Rapide, they'd debated about the shape of the fuselage, worried that the sharp nose and rear-facing propellers might look too much like a Wraith Dart. She had argued that the two short winglets that jutted from the plane's nose made it look different enough, that the design's other advantages outweighed the potential risk; now she just hoped she hadn't misjudged things completely.

"I'm Yustyna Tan," Tan said, her voice admirably controlled. She nodded toward Mel. "Mel Hocken. That's our airplane — we've come up from the capital, from the new settlement there —"

"Wraith worshipper!" the young man who had spoken before said, and spat. "Kill them now."

"We're not Wraith worshippers," Mel began, and Tan interrupted.

"What are you talking about? We're from the capital, we're

part of the settlement that's come back since the Wraith left."

"Then what's this thing?" The old man waved his rifle at the Rapide. "Where did you get it, if not from the Wraith?"

"We traded for it," Tan snapped. "Dug salvage for two years, and traded for it, so we could find any other survivors. People like you!"

"The general radioed that there was an overflight." That was a dark-skinned man, who had been silent until now. "They did say it didn't look Wraith — sure didn't sound like them."

"We had an engine problem," Tan said. "So we landed here to fix it."

"There's nothing left in the capital except the Wraith and Wraith worshippers," another young man said.

"There haven't been Wraith in the capital for ten years," Tan said.

"Traded with who?" the old man asked. "Not even the Genii make flying machines."

"With the Lanteans," Tan answered. "With Atlantis —"

All around them, the strangers froze, and then rifles lifted. "I told you they were Wraith worshippers," the young man said. "Just shoot them now."

"We are not Wraith worshippers," Tan began, her voice rising, and the dark-skinned man lifted a hand.

"Wait a minute, now. Just wait a minute. Whatever this thing it, it's not Wraith work. Look at it."

"So they changed things so we wouldn't suspect," someone said, from the back of the group.

The old man shook his head. "The Wraith wouldn't bother." He stared at them, frowning, and Mel held her breath. If the old man decided they were Wraith spies, there wasn't much they could do to save themselves. Maybe she could throw herself into the man closest to her, knock him off balance long enough for Tan to run, but she herself wouldn't survive, and there wasn't much of anywhere for Tan to run… It was better than letting herself be shot, but that wasn't saying much. She was just glad she hadn't said she was from Atlantis herself.

"Let the general decide," the dark man said.

"We can't bring them to the mine," the younger man protested, and the old man shook his head again, more decisively this time.

"Yar's right. We'll bring them back with us."

"That's bringing the Wraith right to us," someone else said.

"They won't be able to follow us on the cliff path," the old man said.

The dark man — Yar — sighed. "They might have trackers."

"Search them," the old man ordered, and Mel stood very still as one of the men went through her pockets. For an instant, she hoped he'd leave her multi-tool, but he emptied her pockets of everything, down to the rubber band she had picked up the last time she was on Atlantis.

"No weapons," he reported. "Just tools."

"Same here," the man who had searched Tan said, and the old man nodded.

"Right. You'll come with us. Do exactly as we say, and nobody gets hurt."

"Our people will be looking for us if we don't report in," Mel said. "We don't want trouble — we came up here hoping to find people — but they won't be happy if anything happens to us."

Yar shrugged. "Then do what Jas says." He gestured with his rifle, and Mel fell into step behind nearest Satedan, Tan following a few steps behind.

"I don't understand," she began, and Mel shrugged.

"Let's hope we can talk some sense into this general of theirs."

"No talking," Yar said, and Mel concentrated on the trail.

Once they reached the general, it shouldn't be that hard to convince him of their good intentions. Surely.

***

"No," McKay said, his voice loud in the earpiece, "no, I don't think it's the transformer because that isn't a transformer. Possibly the *modulator* could be redesigned to either accommodate lower power transfers as needed or a larger heat sink could be installed."

Radek took a deep breath. "Ok, power modulator, then. And, yes, it seems as though it needs to be redesigned, as Mel — Colonel Hocken — needs to be able to fly at low power for extended periods."

"Yes, ok, I'll work on that. But as a temporary fix, you should be able to drill holes in the fuselage to allow more air flow and thus more cooling."

"I had thought of that," Radek said. "And I will probably do that if we can't find another answer — or if you don't come up with something by the time the plane is back here."

"Which I may very well have done, yes," Rodney said. "I just — look, the timing's not wonderful, ok? But I'll see what I can do."

"Thank you," Radek said, and cut the connection.

"Any luck?" Ronon asked, and Radek managed a nod.

"Yes. He will work on the problem. And we have stopgap measures if he doesn't produce new transformers — modulators, whatever, it is the same thing regardless of what Rodney says — right away." Radek gave a rueful smile. "It will bother him, and he will work on it all night, and you know that first thing in the morning we will receive a message saying he has fixed the problem and why didn't we just wait for him to fix it? But he will get the job done."

"Will it work?" Ronon lowered his voice so that neither Wood nor the two Satedans drinking tea at the far end of the lobby could hear. "I mean, no disrespect to McKay, but he isn't always right."

He just thinks he is. Radek swallowed the words because they were no longer true. Rodney had changed during the years he'd spent on Atlantis, become braver and more thoughtful — *in another man, I would call it humility,* Radek thought, *but Rodney was never humble.* Rather, he considered the consequences more thoroughly, without losing the ability to make those startling jumps of something that wasn't logic at all, but unconstrained genius. "No, but when he is wrong, it's because he skipped over something simple to get to the part he thought was interesting. He's gotten better about that. And this is his project. He was very pleased to have figured out to adapt the stripped-down generator to the Rapide. He won't allow it to fail."

Ronon nodded slowly. "And you think you can get them back here before nightfall?"

"As long as the transformer cools completely, and there's no reason it wouldn't."

"I wish we had those satellites everyone is always talking about," Ronon said. It was so much what Radek had been thinking himself that he blinked in surprise. "Or Atlantis's sensors."

"Yes, I agree. If there are going to be regular flights, some better weather forecasting system is required." Satellites would be the easiest thing, Radek thought. You wouldn't even need rockets, just place them in orbit from a puddle jumper —

"Mr. Dex?" Wood frowned at her console, working the dials. There was a note in her voice that made the hair rise at the back of Radek's neck.

"Yeah?" Ronon was at her side in three long strides, and Radek followed.

"The Rapide was supposed to check in fifteen minutes ago,"

Wood said. "Nothing. And I've been trying to raise them for the last five minutes, and I'm not getting any answer."

"Keep trying," Ronon said, and looked at Radek.

"It's possible that they had to switch off the generator completely," Radek said, "though why they would have to do that now, I can't think. But without standby power, they don't have radio."

"Not a weak signal, anything like that?" Ronon asked.

"I don't think so," Wood answered. "We had ten-of-ten reception every other time, and nothing's changed."

"Ok. Keep trying to raise them," Ronon said. He reached for the spare radio, switched it on. "I'm calling the capital."

"We don't know anything," Radek began, not quite wanting to say *do you really want to upset the governor now*, and Ronon shrugged as though he'd read the thought.

"I was thinking we might be able to send a drone."

"That is a good thought," Radek said.

Ronon adjusted the radio's frequency settings, and Radek reached for his tablet again, calling up the transformer schematics. They needed to be able to handle more power, but couldn't be more than a few centimeters larger, or very much heavier at all…

"Zelenka."

Radek looked up at Ronon's call. "Yes?"

"Still no answer from Hocken. And your sergeant says the drones can't make it to the Plateau even if they use the most direct route. Not enough fuel. I'm going to ask Atlantis to send a puddle jumper."

"Yes," Radek said again, feeling the familiar crawl of fear down his spine. "Yes, that would be wise."

***

It was only a couple of hours before the puddle jumper eased into its landing spot in front of the power station, but Ronon had to grit his teeth to keep from asking where they'd been. He knew that they'd come as fast as they could, but it might not be fast enough, not when they didn't know what had happened to the Rapide... The back of the puddle jumper came down, and Lorne emerged, followed by one of the Marine sergeants.

"Ronon! Any news?"

"Still nothing." Ronon glanced at the sun, dropping fast now toward the treetops. "We've got about two hours of daylight left."

"Plenty of time," Lorne said. "And the good news is, we don't really need it. The sensors will pick up life signs even in the dark." He paused. "I brought a response team just in case."

Ronon could see them, three more Marines in full battledress sitting patiently inside the jumper. "Yeah. Couldn't hurt. Though —Tan said they'd spotted signs of a settlement, but that was below the cliff edge. It's a big cliff."

Lorne glanced sideways at the Falls, the spray at the top just catching the last of the sunlight. "So I see."

Movement caught Ronon's eye, and he looked around to see Zelenka coming briskly toward them, tablet tucked under his arm. "Are we ready?" he asked. "Let us not waste the light."

For a moment, Ronon considered telling him to stay, or at least to put on armor. Except that the scientists hadn't brought full military gear, and there wasn't time to find something to borrow that would fit him. He realized abruptly that Lorne was waiting for him to make the decision, and nodded. "Let's go."

The puddle jumper rose quickly up the cliff face, Lorne taking it close enough to the Falls that the edge of the spray struck the windscreen. They emerged into the last of the sunlight, and Lorne adjusted the controls to leave them hovering over the top of the Falls. To the north, Ronon saw, the Tellhart narrowed toward the horizon, its wide surface mirroring the sun; to the west, there was a clearing and more thick woods — the Ezes had come down the Tellhart's western bank, he remembered. "Hocken landed on the east side."

"Yeah." Lorne frowned at the controls, talking to them the way the Ancestors had done, and a moment later a map appeared, a light flashing in its center. "Ok, sensors are picking up the Rapide's beacon."

He turned the jumper eastward, putting the sun at their backs. They were flying over another open clearing, a long meadow that spread between the cliff's edge and the forest to the north, and the sun caught something small and white in the distance. Ronon pointed.

"There."

"I see it." Lorne looked down at his controls again. "I'm not picking up any life signs."

"None at all?" Zelenka asked sharply, leaning forward between the pilots' seats.

Lorne shook his head. "Nothing."

As they came closer, it was unmistakably the Rapide, sitting alone and silent in the sea of grass. Lorne circled twice, then looped toward the forest and back again, and finally set the jumper down neatly next to the Rapide. Ronon levered himself out of his seat, drawing his weapon, and joined the Marines at the rear door. The door lifted, letting in the peppery smell of the grass and a fainter scent of pitch from the conifers, but nothing moved in the fading light.

"Gordon, Wallace," the sergeant said. "Check it out."

"Sir." The two Marines moved forward at a crouch, the third and the sergeant moving up to cover them. Wallace and Gordon split up, circled the Rapide, and then Gordon crouched at the base of the open hatch while Wallace sprinted up the stairs. He reappeared a moment later, shaking his head.

"Nothing, Major."

"I would like at least to take a look at the airplane," Zelenka said, and ducked past the Marines. Ronon followed more slowly, scanning the area around the Rapide.

"What do you think's happened?" Lorne asked quietly.

"I don't know." Ronon walked to the Rapide's tail, staring south toward the edge of the cliff, and Lorne followed.

"If somebody did capture them, you'd be able to track them, right?"

Ronon shook his head. The grass was thick and coarse and tremendously resilient; an army could have passed without leaving signs. "There's no track where the plane landed. People aren't going to leave a trail."

"Damn it." Lorne turned to look back at the trees. "If they were taken — by who, and where did they come from? There wasn't any sign of people in those woods."

"I don't know." If Hocken and Tan were prisoners — Ronon was betting on that. Why else would they leave the plane without letting the base at the Falls know where they were going? If they were prisoners, they had to be heading for some settlement, and the only settlement they knew about was the one Tan had reported, at the old mine not far from the base of the cliff. Unless they came from the woods? "How far do the sensors reach? The ones on the jumper."

Lorne considered. "We'd have picked up anyone within about a seven mile radius. Maybe further."

That would reach well beyond the cliff's edge as well as into the forest. And they'd flown into the forest for some Lantean miles, which made it unlikely any attackers could have gotten themselves and their prisoners out of sensor range. And there were always paths down the sides of the Plateau. Not easy ones, but certainly manageable even with prisoners. "I'm going to see if I can spot anything."

He turned away without waiting for an answer, brushing carefully through the tall grass. Behind the plane, he found some stems that looked scuffed and bruised, marked, he guessed, by the landing; he cast from side to side until he found the edges of that track, then straightened, looking for signs that something smaller had passed this way. The grass swayed gently in the rising breeze, and he caught a flash of disturbed ground between two clumps of grass. There was another beyond it, and a third, and that one bore the distinctive marks of the Lanteans' military boots. Hocken, at least, had come this way.

He lost the trail before he reached the edge, and a quick search along the top in the fading light offered several possible paths down the cliff face. None of them looked more likely than the others, and he straightened, baring his teeth in frustration, then touched his radio.

"Major. Looks like they went down the cliff, but I can't tell where."

"Can they do that?" Lorne asked, and Ronon had to remind himself again that the Lanteans knew very little about Sateda outside the capital.

"Probably. There are dozens of known trails, and probably a lot more that never made it onto any maps. Especially around the mines." Ronon started back toward the Rapide. "Question is, do we go after them now, or wait until morning?"

"We don't have any idea where they're going," Lorne said.

"Nothing on the plane?"

Lorne shook his head. "Nothing helpful. All their maps are still there, and their rations — and what's left of their lunch, for that matter. Zelenka says the engine cowlings were opened to cool everything, and nobody's touched anything inside."

"Weapons?"

"They only carried a couple of pistols," Lorne said. "Both

missing, but the spare magazines are still here."

None of which was proof that Hocken and Tan were still together — he'd only found the marks of Hocken's boots. But two groups seemed vanishingly unlikely. And none of it gave them any idea where the strangers might be taking them. He wasn't going to try to track them even a little way down the cliff in the growing twilight. "We need to figure out where they've been taken — where they've gone."

Lorne nodded. "Yeah. I hate leaving them, but you're right. I told Zelenka to pull the drives from the cameras, maybe there will be something there that'll give us a clue."

"That settlement Tan said they saw."

"Yeah."

"I agree." Ronon looked back at the cliff, wishing he could carry on — even if he could camp at the top of the cliff and wait there for morning, he'd feel more as though he was doing something. But that was a stupid idea, especially when they could use that time to make better plans. "Let's go."

CHAPTER FOUR

IT HAD been a long and difficult walk down the cliff face, though once they'd gone a few hundred meters, ropes and handholds appeared, carefully colored to blend in with the rock face. It was certainly a good way to discourage any escape attempts, Mel thought. She had been too busy concentrating on her footing to think of making a break for it, and the thought of trying to climb that same steep face while the Satedans were shooting at her was thoroughly discouraging. But surely it wouldn't come to that. Once they had a chance to explain the situation, to prove that they weren't Wraith worshippers... She slipped on a patch of moss and Tan steadied her.

"Do we try to get away?" she whispered, and Mel shook her head.

"Not yet —"

"No talking," one of the men said, glaring, and Mel lifted her hands.

"Ok."

They had reached the edge of the woods, passing through the first of what looked like several linked clearings, and Mel saw the stack of cut timber that they had seen from the air. There was the elevated wooden sluice, water flowing steadily away from the mine, and then they had reached the cleared area in front of the mine itself. She recognized the buildings she had seen from the air, though up close they didn't look quite as deserted. Yes, the doors gaped and there was no glass in the windows, but it looked as though work was going on inside those battered shells. Up a graveled slope, the entrance to the mine itself gaped wide, but to her surprise, the group's leader took them to the smaller of the two buildings to the left of the entrance. From the look of it, it had been some kind of administrative building, single-story, with a set of smaller rooms off a narrow lobby; the Satedans had shored up the walls and roof and replaced one of the rooms' doors with a crudely-forged set of bars. The old man motioned them inside, and ostentatiously closed it with a padlock the size of his fist. There were no windows, and the only light came from an oil lantern, hung on the far side of the hall. There was a sturdy-looking wooden cot and what looked like a rolled-up mattress, but no other furniture.

"Wait a minute," Mel said. "What about us?"

"That's up to the general," he said, and turned away.

Mel leaned against the bars, watching him walk out of sight. There was a man with a rifle at the end of the hall, but that was the only guard she could see. An advantage, maybe, she thought, except that there was still that cliff to climb before they could get back to the Rapide.

"There used to be a window here," Tan said, from the back of the cell. "But they boarded it up. If we could pry it open —"

"There's a guard at the end of the hall," Mel said. "He'd hear." She moved back from the door, positioning herself where she couldn't be seen, but she would be able to tell as soon as someone moved down the corridor.

"Not to mention they haven't left us anything to pry with. Unless we could break up this cot. And we'd have to get back up the cliff."

"Yeah." They could try hiding in the forest, of course, Mel thought, but the locals would know the ground a lot better than they did. "What's going on, can you tell?"

"It sounds like they just don't know anyone's come back," Tan answered. She moved closer, lowering her voice. "And if that's true, we ought to be fine, we just need to convince them. Though I would have thought they'd have picked up some of our broadcasts by now."

Cai had had the radio operators sending out general messages several times a day, hoping to reach surviving communities. Mel had doubted it would do much good, but Tan had disagreed. Lots of outlying towns and even farms had always provided their own power; she would certainly have kept checking the radios just in case.

"Not much good reception in the mountains," Mel began, and stopped as something moved in the hall. "They're coming back. You better do the talking."

"Let's hope they'll listen," Tan said nervously.

The hall grew brighter as the newcomers approached, and a tall woman hung two more lanterns on the wall, while a dark man with his braided hair pulled back into a loose tail made his way to the bars. "Right. Who are you people, and where do you come from?"

"My name's Yustina Tan," Tan answered. "And this is Mel Hocken. We're from the capital." Mel could see the stranger pull back, but Tan went on as though she hadn't noticed. "Who are you?"

For a second, Mel thought he wasn't going to answer, but then he said, "Janosi Lek. And I'm surprised you're admitting it. There's nothing in the capital but Wraith worshippers."

"That's not true," Tan said. "There haven't been Wraith in the capital for years — not since the Stargate was reopened. We've started coming back — Satedans who managed to get off world. We're starting to rebuild, with the help of the Lanteans."

"Now I know you're lying," Lek said. "Atlantis. Everyone knows that Atlantis is a trap, a Wraith lie —"

"What?" Mel couldn't stop herself, and Tan made a strangled sound.

"The Lanteans have fought the Wraith from the moment they arrived here! Their people have died with us and for us — they defeated Queen Death when she would have united all the Wraith to enslave all the humans who were still free. How dare you say that they are Wraith worshippers?"

Lek's tone was conciliatory. "I know that is what you have been told, and many have believed it, but we have it on good authority that 'Atlantis' is a trick, to lure survivors into the open so that they can be culled."

"But I've met the Lanteans," Tan protested. "Many of them —"

"I'm from Atlantis," Mel said. It was a risk, she knew, but it was the quickest way she could think of to cut through the confusion.

"Impossible!" Lek took a step back, as though he'd been struck.

"It's true," Mel said.

"You've seen Wraith aircraft before," Tan said. "There were pictures of their Darts posted before the great culling. Ask the people who captured us, our plane is nothing like that."

"It is different," someone said, from the crowd, and Lek paused.

"We'll put it to the general when he gets back. In the meantime — bring them food and water, but keep them here."

There was a murmur of agreement, and Tan said, "Can we have a lamp, please?"

Lek hesitated, but shook his head. "We'll leave this one in the hall."

"But —" Tan began, but they were gone. She sighed. "That could have gone better."

"It could have gone worse," Mel said.

"Well, all right, they haven't shot us," Tan agreed, with a crooked smile. She turned to the cot, and unrolled the mattress, releasing a cloud of dust. "Ugh. Though if we have to sleep here, shooting might be preferable."

"Any idea who this general of theirs might be?" Mel slapped the mattress a few times, decided that it wasn't going to get any better, and seated herself, resting her back against the wall. It had been a long haul down the cliff and through the forest, and the more she could recover, the better.

Tan seemed to have the same idea, and settled next to her. "I don't know. This wasn't a military area before the Wraith — these mines were pretty well played out, and some of them had actually closed. Though I suppose if a unit was retreating from the capital, this might be a reasonable place to hide. Or maybe they came over the Spur from the power plant. I'm pretty sure there was a unit stationed there. These mines are deep, the Wraith sensors can't reach them there."

"Makes sense," Mel agreed, and rested her head against the wall.

After a while — it was impossible to tell how much time had passed, since the miners had taken their watches — a woman arrived with a tray that held two wooden bowls and a wooden pitcher. She slid it into the cell under the watchful eye of two guards, and Tan collected it. There were two cups and two spoons, Mel saw, and the bowls were filled with a thick stew. She tasted it cautiously, and decided it was nearly identical to the food she got in the capital, bland but filling. The pitcher contained a dark liquid that tasted like pine needles, but it was the only thing they had to drink, and Mel quickly downed two cups. Tan sniffed at it and made a face.

"Mountain tea. I've never liked it."

"We need to stay hydrated," Mel pointed out, and Tan sighed.

"I know."

They ate in silence, and left the tray with the emptied dishes by the door of the cell. It had to be getting late, Mel thought, and wondered where the general was, or where he had gone that it took him this much time to make his appearance. Ronon and the others would be looking for them, too, and they'd already radioed them enough information that a team in a puddle jumper could find the mine. The trick was going to be making sure nobody got shot by accident.

***

Apparently conference rooms on Sateda looked very much like conference rooms on Earth. Radek poured himself yet another cup of coffee and turned back to the polished table. The wood was redder then most Earth timbers, and the pronounced grain was almost black, but everything else could have fit unnoticeably into every place he had ever worked. The harsh electric light beat down on them all, washing out the images on laptops and tablets and emphasizing that everyone was exhausted. He rubbed his own chin, feeling the stubble, and scowled at the map clumsily overlaid on the images sent back before the Rapide had been forced to land.

"So we are in agreement that this is the Wild Blue mine? Here where the clearing is?"

"Above the clearing," Tec said. He had worked in several of the Spur's mines before the Wraith, driving steam-powered diggers. "About two of your miles? The ground opens up again there — you can see what's left of the mine head in this shot." He touched his tablet, dragging the image from forest to rocky ground that revealed two large wooden buildings. "There used to be a steam plant on the other side, but that was dismantled when the mine was sold, back in — well, at least five years before the Wraith came."

Radek studied the map Kos had found that showed the

Spur's mines and their main tunnels. The Satedans had burrowed deep into the rock, opening a spiderweb of connecting lines beneath the mountain, some of which seemed to reach all the way to their side of the Spur. The thought of digging that out essentially by hand, men with picks and shovels carefully setting gunpowder into holes drilled into the blind end of a tunnel… Cheyenne Mountain had at least been hollowed out by machines.

"We've decided that Hocken and Tan are probably at the Wild Blue?" Lorne said, sounding doubtful, and Ronon shrugged. He was standing by the sideboard as though he couldn't bear to sit down any longer.

"It's where we should start. The tracks led to the cliff edge, and that's the nearest place they're likely to have been taken. There were ways down."

"I agree," Radek said. "So we have to assume that they went with someone, presumably from the settlement. And not willingly, or they would have let us know."

"If there are survivors, they're most likely living in the mine itself," Tec said. "Some of these upper galleries are going to be dry enough to be comfortable."

"If they're being held prisoner," Lorne said, "it's going to be hell to dig them out of guarded tunnels."

Ronon nodded. "Maybe they're not prisoners."

"Then they should have radioed," Lorne said.

"Yeah," Ronon said. "So. If they're prisoners, how do we get them out? Besides killing everybody?"

"That is probably worth avoiding," Radek murmured, and saw Ronon give a fleeting smile. "Surely this is most likely some sort of misunderstanding. The people who walked down from the Plateau didn't know that anyone else had survived, and were rightfully wary of strangers."

"The miners were always a stubborn bunch," Tec said. "You

can't threaten them, it just makes them meaner."

Lorne shook his head, studying his laptop again. "I don't like the idea of having to go into these tunnels after them. There's just too much chance the miners could use our people as hostages."

"What about gas?" Ronon asked. "Shock grenades?"

"I only brought a little tear gas," Lorne said. "Three, four canisters. And I don't want to use shock grenades underground. Too much chance of bringing the ceiling down."

"That would be a bad idea," Radek agreed. "Perhaps we could bargain? Trade?"

"Maybe —" Ronon began, and there was a knock at the door.

Radek looked over his shoulder as Kos pushed the door open, a thick book tucked into the crook of her other arm.

"I knew we had to have a copy," she said, and dropped it onto the table with a satisfying thud. Radek had learned to recognize the Institute of Mines' seal since he'd come here, but the words were unfamiliar. "This is the map book that covers the Spur. All the diggings, plus the service tunnels and rail lines, all in one book."

Radek reached for it, but Ronon was quicker, flipping rapidly through the pages. "Yeah. Here's the Wild Blue."

Radek moved to look past his shoulder, pushing his glasses back into a comfortable position. There had to be ten pages of maps, maybe more, level after level stacked on top of each other, all with dozens of tunnels reaching back into the mountain, and he shook his head in dismay. "This is a labyrinth."

"Odds are there aren't very many miners," Ronon said. "These weren't big settlements before the Wraith, and not everybody will have stayed. Not to mention that we haven't seen any fields or anything like that. So a lot of this is empty space."

"I agree," Lorne said.

"We'll need copies of the maps," Radek said. "Everyone who goes should have their own copy, in case they get separated."

"I found the office pantograph," Kos said. "I think it still works."

"We can image and scan them to tablets, too," Lorne began, and Radek looked up.

"We should have both, just in case. As many copies as Ms. Kos can make for us. We may not have the option of tablets." He shook his head. "I hope getting lost is the worst of our problems."

"The doc's right," Lorne said. "We really don't want to try to fight down there."

Ronon nodded. "Yeah. I say we leave at first light."

Radek pulled the book closer to him, tuning out the discussion of logistics. If that was the Wild Blue's main level seen from above, was that a tunnel that ran all the way to the western side of the Spur? He nudged Kos, who turned to look where he was pointing. "What is this? Does it come out on our side?"

"It seems to," she said, and took the book from him, flipping pages to consult what had to be a map key. "Yes — yes, that's the old rail access. They used to bring some of the goods to this side of the Spur, before the east branch of the rail line was completed."

"Rail access?" Ronon asked, and Kos pointed.

"Dr. Zelenka reminded me. This is not far from here, there's a cartage road."

"A back door?" Lorne said, and Ronon nodded again, considering.

"Yeah. That changes things."

"I agree," Lorne said.

"Let's play this like Teyla would," Ronon said, with another fleeting grin. "Major, you take your Marines and knock on the front door. Find out if Hocken and Tan are just visiting, and if we can get them back without trouble. If not, see if you can spot where they're being held, and I'll bring a team through on foot and see if I can't bring them out the back way."

That was exactly the sort of plan at which Teyla had proved herself an expert, Radek thought. And that was always a good thing. "I will go with Major Lorne," he said aloud. The others looked at him, and he shrugged. "I am not particularly threatening."

"Good idea," Ronon said. For a second, the mask slipped, and Radek caught of glimpse of the same worry that haunted them all. Were Hocken and Tan guests or prisoners, alive or dead? There was nothing they could do until morning.

***

It was getting late, and the temperature inside the cell was dropping steadily. The woman who took away their dinner tray brought a couple of coarse wool blankets, and Mel and Tan huddled into them, sitting shoulder to shoulder on the cot for greater warmth. After a while, they wrapped one blanket around their shoulders and pulled the other up over to their chins, and the shared body heat inside the cocoon made the situation almost bearable. Mel leaned her head against the wall, and drifted into a doze.

She woke when Tan elbowed her, saying quietly, "Someone's coming."

Mel straightened, loosening the blankets so that they could move quickly if they had to. "Do you know what time it is?"

Tan shook her head. "Late."

Mel could hear voices in the hall, two men, but she couldn't make out the words. A few moments later, though, a stranger came into view, and leaned against the bars of the cell. He was an older man, broad-faced, with graying hair and a straggle of gray beard, a military-cut jacket hanging loosely on his shoulders, as though it had been made for him when he was younger and heavier.

"So. You say you came up from the capital."

Mel glanced at Tan, who gave a fractional shrug: Mel's call, then. She disentangled herself from the blankets and moved toward the door herself, Tan following at her shoulder. "That's right. The provisional government there is looking for survivors."

"The capital was taken over by Wraith worshippers," the man said. "There's no one trustworthy there."

Tan made a sudden startled noise. "Wait, he —"

She stopped abruptly. Mel gave her a wary look, but she shook her head.

"Nothing. Never mind."

The big man sighed, and a wry smile crossed his face. "Well, it's not that big a community. All right, you know me. And I know you. You're the photographer, Tan."

Tan didn't answer, eyeing him unhappily, and Mel looked from one to the other. "Would one of you like to fill me in?"

"He's — you lied to them," Tan said, to the stranger. "You told them we were Wraith worshippers. You kept them from joining us."

He lifted both hands. "Keep your voice down. You're not in the best position here either."

"Who is he?" Mel said, to Tan, and the photographer controlled herself with an effort.

"This is Evrast Mar. He's the general they were talking about. He's been telling the governor that he's 'exploring' the country up here, looking for salvage and survivors, and all the time he's been —" She broke off abruptly. "I don't know what he's been doing, except keeping these people from leaving and finding things out for themselves."

"That's not entirely true," Mar said. "I've been keeping them safe since the Wraith attacked, and I'm still keeping them safe."

"Not if you're not telling them the truth about Satedans returning," Mel said.

"It's still safer here than it is in the capital," Mar said. "The Wraith will come back, and we don't have enough of anything left to have a hope of defending ourselves when they do." He shook his head. "But, we won't argue about that. I've got a deal for you. You keep your mouths shut about the capital, and I'll tell my people you aren't Wraith worshippers. I'll even take you with me when I leave."

"And if we don't?" Mel asked.

Mar shook his head. "The miners up here really don't like Wraith worshippers."

Mel swore under her breath. "I already told them I was Lantean."

"So you exaggerated a little. You probably traded with the Lanteans for that plane, right?" Mar grinned. "Do it, and I promise you, you'll be back in the capital in no time at all."

"You're leaving out something important," Mel said. "There's a Lantean team at the Narmoth Falls, and they'll be looking for us. They know we're down on the Plateau —"

"But they don't know you're here," Mar interrupted.

"They'll figure that out."

"Maybe, maybe not."

"And they won't stop looking." Mel went on as if he hadn't spoken. "You have to have realized that by now. We don't leave our people behind."

"I don't need to keep you forever," Mar said. "I don't want to keep you forever. I need — one more week, maybe two at the outside. You don't want to die over that, do you? Just cooperate, and everybody walks away safe and unharmed."

Mel glanced at Tan. Mar was right, the miners were already half convinced that they were Wraith worshippers, and Wraith worshippers didn't live long on Sateda — she couldn't even blame them for that, not after what they'd been through. They'd already failed to convince the miners, and if Mar spoke out against them, they would be in even worse trouble than they were now. She heard Tan heave a sigh, and shook her own head. "All right. We'll play along."

"You won't regret it," Mar said.

Mel wished she believed that.

"Kormin!" Mar took a step back from the bars. "It's all right, there's been a misunderstanding. These people are friends."

"Yeah?" The guard came into view, looking doubtful, but his expression eased as Mar kept talking.

"That's right, they're from up-country, they were taken in by the Wraith worshippers, but now they've seen the light. They'll be staying with us for a bit, until we're sure the worshippers can't follow them."

"What about that aircraft up there?"

It was a good question, Mel thought, but Mar didn't even blink.

"We'll just leave it, and lie low for a few days. It'll be a mystery!" He shrugged. "At some point, I imagine they'll come and take it away, and then things can get back to normal. But in the meantime, let's get our guests inside."

"Wait a minute," Mel said. "We're fine here."

"It's much safer inside the mine," Mar said. His voice took on a faint edge. "And, of course, it's proof of good faith. Let's go."

There was no point in further protest. Mar and several guards led them through the mine's open mouth, and then down a spiral of ever-narrowing tunnels, lit by widely-spaced electric lamps. So they had to have a generator somewhere, Mel thought, and that will be something for the jumper's infrared sensors to home in on. Though if it was far enough underground to fool the Wraith, the jumper might not pick it up, either. She concentrated on remembering the turns, hoping she'd be able to find her way back to the surface, but all the tunnels looked very much alike, the same dark gray rock roughly hewn out into corridors with arched ceilings. At least the relatively dim light would work in their favor, if they could get away, but she had no real confidence that she'd be able to remember the path correctly. Still, if they could follow the miners, surely they could eventually find the entrance. Of course, that meant they'd have to get away first.

They finally stopped at a wooden door that, when unlocked, proved to open on an unexpectedly comfortable room. The stone walls were hung with strips of pale fabric, and there was an electric bulb hanging from a cable just inside the door. There was a wide bed at the back of the room, half hidden by shadows and a draped curtain, and a table and stools toward the front. There was an electric heater as well, a spiral coil glowing red behind its protective bars, and the room was surprisingly warm.

"Right, then," Mar said, rubbing his hands together. "Get some sleep, and we'll talk more in the morning."

"Hang on," Mel began, but the door closed behind them with a very solid-sounding thud. She listened, and heard the distinct click of a key turning in the lock. "Damn it."

Tan had her arms wrapped around herself as though she was cold. "We're locked in?"

Mel tested the latch, gently at first, and then putting her full weight on it. "Yeah."

"Lovely." Tan dropped onto the nearest stool, hunching her shoulders as though she were cold. After a moment, Mel rested a consoling hand on her back.

"It'll be all right. Atlantis will send someone for us — Ronon knows where we were, and they know what we saw.

They'll be here in the morning." She looked around the room again, and spotted the water jug and a stack of pottery cups set on a shelf opposite the heater. She poured a cup for each of them, glad to see that it wasn't the mountain tea Tan had complained about before, and returned to sit down beside the other woman, pressing a cup into her hands. Tan took it with a nod of thanks, and sipped carefully.

"If I could get hold of a stiff piece of wire," Mel said, "I think I could get that lock open."

"There's probably a guard right outside," Tan said. "Or not far off, anyway."

Mel shrugged. "We need a flashlight anyway. We take out the guard, we get a light and at least one weapon."

"Against how many miners?" Tan sounded skeptical, but Mel could feel that she was shaking less. "Wouldn't it be better to wait and see what your people do?"

"Probably."

"Anyway, it doesn't look like they've left any wire lying around."

"No." Mel sighed. "I just — what do you know about this General Mar, anyway? Can we trust him?"

"He was regular army before the Wraith," Tan said. "Mountain troops, I think? He had one of the sector commands, though he wasn't a politician, not like Kell. He was posted to the west, I think, but he was in the capital when the Wraith came." She frowned as though she was trying to make sense of memories she hadn't recalled for years. "It — I think the story I heard was that he couldn't get back to his command, and the Wraith managed to wipe out the northern command in a lucky strike, so he took over there instead. He met up with some disorganized units, or what was left of them, but realized there wasn't anything he could do to stop the culling. He fought a rearguard action and retreated up the Spur and then east along the edge of the Plateau, managed to hide out there until the culling stopped. Or at least that's what he told the governor."

"And we can't trust any of that anymore," Mel said. "Right. He could have been here the whole time."

Tan nodded. "It wouldn't surprise me if he was. That might explain why he didn't bring more people into the capital with him. And why he didn't set up a regular radio link."

"So what's he doing here that he doesn't want Cai to know about?"

"I can't imagine," Tan answered. "I mean, these are silver mines, but — silver's not that important right now. We need iron and coal a lot more than we need silver."

I bet we'll find out, Mel thought, but decided not to say that out loud. "Let's get some sleep. If Ronon shows up in the morning, I want to be ready."

***

They clustered around the puddle jumper in the chill pre-dawn light, maps and tablets out to go over the plan one last time. Radek listened with half an ear, knowing that he knew his part, and knowing, too, that if something did go wrong — as it probably would — the plan would be out the window and they'd be improvising instead. Luckily, both Ronon and Lorne were good at making things up on the fly. The trouble was, there wasn't much they could actually do in the way of planning: they knew entirely too little about what was waiting for them at the Wild Blue.

"So if you run into trouble, pull back and keep them busy at the front of the mine," Ronon said, "and I'll walk my team in from the west entrance and try to get our people out that way."

Radek couldn't help glancing around at the group gathered on the tarmac. They had agreed that Kasper would stay with the radio, and that only left Ronon, Corporal Wood, and the four Satedans to perform the rescue. Even assuming that the Satedans had all of necessity learned to fight, it was hard to feel that the odds would be in their favor. On the other hand, the main search team was only himself and Lorne and three Marines, and, while he would be the last person to argue that the Marines' pride was misplaced, there was no way to know how many people were living in the mine. This was definitely a moment for negotiations, not force, if at all possible.

"Yeah," Lorne said. "If it comes to that, I'll try to put somebody into the mine, so they can find Hocken and Tan and then hook up with you."

Ronon grunted agreement. "Keep us up on what you're doing, ok?"

"Will do," Lorne answered. "All right, everybody, load up."

The jumper rose almost silently up the edge of the Plateau, breaking into the sunlight as it neared the top of the waterfall. It was an astonishingly beautiful view, the sun rising ahead of them, the spray haloing the cliff, and Radek saw the Marines nudging and pointing. The Rapide was where they had left it, the white fuselage standing out against the dark grass. Lorne circled twice, dividing his attention between the scanners and the ground below, then shook his head.

"Still no sign of Hocken and Tan. No indication that they've been back to the plane."

And if they had been, surely they would have used the radio. Radek swallowed the words, not wanting to blurt out the obvious, said instead, "Ronon believed they were taken down the cliff."

"Yeah." Lorne eased the jumper forward, losing altitude so that he was only a few meters above the grass. "Let's see if we can find this Wild Blue mine."

Radek leaned forward as Lorne brought the jumper to hover alongside the cliff face. It was more deeply fissured than he had expected, and fractionally less steep, with unexpected ledges, and he caught a glimpse of what looked like a strand of rope about three meters down from the cliff top. "Look there," he said, pointing, and saw Lorne nod.

"Yeah, I see it. It looks like there's a path, all right." He brought the jumper alongside as he spoke, carefully tracing the series of switchbacks until they were hovering just above the treetops.

"Sir," one of the Marines said crisply. "Permission to drop down and look for tracks?"

Lorne considered for a moment, then shook his head. "Sorry, Peebles. We'll stick together for now. They have to have been heading for the mine."

"Sir," Peebles said, and settled back into her place. She was the one who was detailed to try to get away, Radek remembered, on the theory that she was small and quick and quiet and extremely tough even by the Marines' standards. He had taken an unarmed combat class from her shortly after arriving on Atlantis, and was still quietly afraid.

"We should be about five kilometers northeast of the mine," Fishman said, in the co-pilot's seat, and Lorne nodded.

"Right. Let's go see what's there."

He lifted the jumper to hover about thirty meters above the treetops, and turned toward the line of mountains. Ahead, the forest stretched unbroken, the dark green foliage waving slightly in their wake. Then a break appeared, and Radek caught his breath, seeing the stacked wood at one edge of the clearing.

"Major —"

"I saw," Lorne said. "Looks like we're on the right track."

"Or at least we are seeing what they saw," Radek said. He leaned forward again as something caught his eye. "And see — there's the sluice they photographed."

"Got it," Lorne said.

"Looks like it leads straight to the mine," Fishman said.

The mine itself was hard to miss, a dark hole at the base of the mountain's steepest face. Lorne circled three times, but the scanners picked up no signs of life. "Of course, I'm not penetrating very far into the rock," he said, "but there's nobody on the surface, not in those buildings or in the woods or up on the slopes. I'm setting down."

He landed the jumper directly in front of the mine opening, where its weapons could cover the slope. Its shields made it impervious to any of the Satedans' weapons, but there was no point, Radek thought, in taking unnecessary chances. He had brought his own body armor out of pessimistic habit, and now he was glad of its weight on his back and shoulders. He crouched by the puddle jumper as the Marines fanned out to examine the buildings, and Peebles reappeared almost at once to report that the largest building had been repaired on the inside.

"It's clean, no obvious signs that anybody's been living there," she reported, "but there's a cell and various rooms and they're all in good shape. Not broken up like the outside."

"A reasonable precaution, if they're afraid of the Wraith," Radek said.

Lorne nodded. "Yeah, I know. Let's keep assuming this is all a mistake."

"The sensors saw nothing in the mine entrance," Radek said. "How far in did they reach?"

"A couple hundred meters, maybe a little more. If I had somebody else with the ATA gene, I'd have them scan from the jumper, give us a heads-up if the miners start to show, but that's Fishman, and I need him with us." Lorne touched his radio. "Narmoth Falls, this is Lorne. We're outside the mine, no sign of our party. We're going in."

"Copy that," Kasper answered. "Ronon is on his way to the western entrance."

Radek reached for his tablet, paged through files until he found the first set of maps for the Wild Blue. "There is a fairly large vestibule before it begins to branch."

"Let's check it out." Lorne raised his voice. "All right, people. Going in."

Fishman took point, switching on his head lamp as well as the light on his P90. The others did the same, taking up positions to follow him, their lights cutting through the empty dark. There was no sign of life here, either, just the rock-strewn floor and rough-hewn walls. Radek looked up, and his head lamp's beam swung across more of the same dark stone. There had been tracks once, running down the middle of the passage, but the rails were missing, and half the wooden ties were broken, or buried under a loose layer of rubble. Salvaged, Radek thought, and said, "Major. Someone has taken these rails."

"Yeah, I see." Lorne had his P90 ready, its light sweeping steadily ahead of him. "Any idea when?"

"Not while the mine was in operation. This would be how they brought ore to the surface. So, yes, I think we can assume someone has been living here."

"Right."

They were almost at the end of the vestibule, and Radek could see three openings that matched his map. The air smelled odd, the rock itself giving off a faint oily odor, but there was movement in it, as though fans were working somewhere in the depths. "The right-hand opening leads to a series of short spurs that are marked as closed," he said. "The left leads to the lower levels via the elevator, and the middle goes on another thousand meters before it branches."

"I'd say either right or middle," Fishman said. "The air's

stronger from the middle section."

"Middle it is," Lorne said and they moved forward.

The darkness closed in around them, the light at the entrance a distant, blinding dot. Radek glanced back once, and the afterimage danced across his vision until his eyes adjusted again to the flashlights. There had been electric lights in this tunnel once; the cables were still in place, but the bulbs were missing, and he wondered if that was the work of refugees or if they had been removed to save money when the mine was partially closed.

The tunnel sloped more steeply now, and for the first time the line of track appeared unbroken. Radek stooped to examine the rails, and straightened, frowning. "No rust. This has been in use recently."

"So we're going in the right direction," Lorne said.

Ahead, the tunnel bent sharply to the left, and Fishman slowed, then eased toward the inside of the curve. The other Marines waved to each other, adjusting their positions to provide cover. Radek edged toward the wall himself, glancing around warily. There were more cables running along the walls here, three rows in parallel, each with its own set of empty light sockets; here and there, wires ran to the floor, ending in square boxes that looked as though they might have been power jacks. Light glinted as he turned his head, the beam of the headlight sweeping over something new and shiny, and he said, "Stop."

He hadn't spoken loudly, but the others froze. Lorne looked back at him. "Problem, Doc?"

"I'm not sure yet." Radek turned his head again to focus on the spark of light. It was another wire, running from the power conduits like all the rest; it entered one of the square boxes, and another wire emerged from the box, running across the width of the tunnel. Whoever had put it there had

done their best to camouflage it, but the wire lay a few centimeters above the surface, just enough to catch an unwary
foot. "Yes. A tripwire, there."

"Right," Lorne said. "Everybody got that?" There was a murmur of agreement, and Fishman, who was closest to it, eased
back a few steps. "Can you see what it's hooked up to, Doc?"

"A moment." Radek slung his P90 and pulled out his flashlight. He let that play along the wire, tracing it across the floor
to the opposite wall, expecting to find an alarm or a packet
of explosives. Instead, the wire ended in a rounded cone that
was made of some dark, unreflective material. Some kind of
rubber, he realized, and that meant it was an insulator, and
that in turn meant that the wire was electrified. Possibly it
was just meant to give a warning, but those cables and the
light fixtures attached to them implied a potentially lethal
power source. "The wire is electrified, I think. It will give at
least a nasty shock."

"Nice," Peebles said, not quite under her breath.

Radek ignored her, considering his options. He needed
something non-conducting to break the wire — well, he had
insulated clippers in his toolkit, but he would have preferred
a rubber mat to stand on, not just rely on the rubber soles of
his shoes. Or something non-conducting to pull the wire out
of the box at the base of the wall: that connection seemed to
be a weak point. He looked around, letting his head lamp's
beam play over the debris that had accumulated against the
tunnel walls. Yes, there was a length of wood, probably from
a broken railroad tie, and he scooped it up, checking carefully to be sure there were no spikes or other bits of metal
still attached. There were none, and he took a breath. "Ok.
Stand back, please, everyone."

"We could just step over it," Fishman said.

"Yeah, we might be coming back this way in a hurry," Lorne

said. "Go ahead, Doc."

Radek crouched to examine the connection, balancing his weight on the balls of his feet, then worked the edge of the stick between the wire and the wall. Sparks flew, and he pulled hard. The wire came loose, and he tapped the wire that stretched across the tunnel. Nothing happened, and he reached into his pocket for the clippers, snipped the wire before he could think too hard about it. The twang of the breaking wire was loud in the silence, but there was no shock or sparks, and he gave a sigh of relief.

"Ok. We should be good now."

"Right," Fishman said, and edged forward along the now-cleared wall, the other Marines following.

"Keep an eye out for any more like that," Lorne said.

They turned the corner to find that the corridor not only divided, but there were several smaller openings in the walls to either side. Fishman and Peebles checked them quickly, and Peebles looked over her shoulder.

"Nothing, sir. Just alcoves."

"Right," Lorne began, eyeing the two branches, and suddenly a light flared inside the left-hand tunnel. Radek threw up his hand to shield his eyes, and a voice from the shadows called, "Hold it right there! Put down your weapons!"

Lorne and the Marines flattened themselves against the walls, and Radek copied them, swearing under his breath. This was what they'd been afraid of, what they'd been expecting, and knowing that they'd made contingency plans didn't actually make it any better.

"Who's there?" Lorne called back. "My name's Lorne, I'm here on behalf of the Satedan Provisional Government. We're looking for two of our people, their plane went down on the Plateau —"

"We know why you're here." The shadow moved forward,

resolved into a man with gray hair dressed in ordinary working clothes. "You're not welcome."

"We'd be happy to leave," Lorne said. "Are our people here? We'll happily take them away."

"We have your people. Leave — now! — and I'll release them to you."

"I'd like to talk to them first," Lorne said. "I need to know that they're all right."

There was a scuffle in the tunnel, and then four more figures separated themselves from the group. Radek could make out Hocken, her hands on her head, and Tan next to her with her hands raised. Two men stood behind them with rifles leveled, and he saw Lorne grimace.

"We don't want any trouble. Just let our people go, and we'll be out of here —"

"No deal. Leave now, and they live. Otherwise…"

"He means it, Major," Hocken called, and ducked as one of the others slapped at her.

"All right!" Lorne re-slung his P90, spread his empty hands. "All right, we'll go. But if you don't turn them over, we're going to come after you."

He took a step backward, and then another. Radek saw Peebles looking for cover — she was the one who was supposed to stay behind, the judoka who could slip through the mine tunnels like a ninja — but she was caught between alcoves, fully in the light. She took a step toward one anyway, and a shot snapped from the tunnel, ricocheting from the ceiling and into the walls.

"Hey!" Lorne yelled, grabbing his P90, and the man in the hallway spoke over him.

"Don't even try it, lady. I see you there."

Peebles lifted her hands and backed away, and Radek swore again. She had been spotted, and none of the others were any closer to shelter. But he was right on the edge of one, and it took only one step to slide into its shadows, clutching his P90 to his chest. He flattened himself against the stone, breathing hard, and saw Lorne's eyes flick over him as he passed the opening. So that was the first thing accomplished, Radek thought, though I'm not exactly the ideal person for the job. But I am here, and Lorne knows I'm here, and I know what I'm supposed to do. Track Hocken and Tan.

The lights of the Atlantis party faded, and a new light appeared: the miners, Radek guessed, making sure that Lorne retreated to the entrance. Luckily the alcove was deeper than it looked, and he eased himself to the back of the space, flattening himself behind a projecting piece of stone. He could hear voices, but couldn't quite make out the words; after a moment, the light faded again, taking the voices with it. And now we wait, he thought. They will come back, and I will follow them. Somehow.

CHAPTER FIVE

THE MINE'S western entrance had been easy enough to find, a dark cavern a third of the way up the rocky slope. Once, Ronon saw, there had been an elevated trestle that brought ore trains down from the entrance at a less precipitous angle; he could trace the line of decaying supports that stretched toward the main rail line. More tracks were visible inside the opening, curving down into the dark, and from the map it looked as though they'd be a good guide if they had to go in. He hoped they wouldn't: fighting underground was bad enough, but when your enemy knew all the back ways and secret passages, it was close to impossible. No, if they had to go in, they had to be sneaky, find Hocken and Tan and slip back out again before anybody knew what they'd done. He glanced at his team, Wood with the smaller portable radio braced against a rock, waiting to hear from Lorne and the main team, the Satedans perched in the sun, talking quietly as though they had nothing better to do than to enjoy the weather.

The radio crackled, and Wood grabbed for headphones and mic. "Wood here. Yes, sir, I'll put him on."

Ronon grimaced, knowing what this had to mean, and Lorne's voice sounded in his ear. "Ronon. No luck with Plan A. Plan B is now a go."

"Ok." Ronon paused, "What's the situation?"

"It's what we were afraid of," Lorne answered. "There is what seems to be a community of miners living in the Wild Blue, and they've taking Hocken and Tan prisoner. They threatened to shoot them, so we withdrew. We're outside the

STARGATE ATLANTIS: THE WILD BLUE

main entrance, trying to re-establish contact."

"Ok." That wasn't great, but it wasn't as bad as it could have been. "Did you manage to get Peebles inside?"

"Negative." Lorne paused. "Dr. Zelenka managed to break off. As far as we know, he's trying to get through to Hocken and Tan."

At least we've got somebody on the inside, Ronon thought. Zelenka was tougher than he looked. "Any idea where they're holding our people?"

"Negative on that as well." Lorne sounded faintly disgusted with himself. "Hopefully Zelenka will get back to us on that. Also, we spotted some tripwires as we got deeper into the mine, likely electrified. Zelenka said they'd probably give a nasty shock."

"Understood," Ronon said. "We're going in."

"Copy that," Lorne said. "We'll radio as soon as we have anything from Zelenka."

"Thanks," Ronon said, and straightened. "All right, people. We're heading in."

The tracks ran along what the maps indicated was a main-level tunnel that seemed to run the full width of the mine. They made their way cautiously along the rails, which were largely intact, though there were enough stones and debris against rails and wooden crossties to suggest that no one had been that way in a while. Ronon took point, keeping his eyes out for the glint of wire or any other booby traps, but there was nothing. After a few hours, they stopped to rest and check the radio; Lorne reported that he could hear them clearly, but that there was no word from Zelenka.

"Not that I expected any," he added. "Not until he finds Hocken, and can check in safely, and that's going to take a while."

If he ever did find a safe place to check in, Ronon thought.

He wasn't going to worry about contacting Zelenka until they got a lot closer to the inhabited parts of the mine. "Got it. We'll keep in touch." He closed the connection, and glanced around the chamber. "Move out."

After another hour of walking, the tracks, which had been going uphill, leveled out, and Kos, who had been charting their progress on the maps copied from the map book back at the Falls, announced that they were now in the mine's working area. They passed a series of tunnels, and then the main tunnel turned slightly south, its walls unbroken. Kos consulted her maps again, and said they were crossing into the earliest sections of the mine. Ahead, the tunnel curved again, the rock walls darker in the beams of their head lamps; there was less debris on the tracks, as though the area had been maintained more recently.

"Careful," Ronon began, and then he saw it, the light of his head lamp sweeping across not stone or open air but a haphazard pile of rubble, piled to block the tracks. "Lights out."

They obeyed instantly and stood for a long moment in the sudden dark, listening for movement on the other side of the barrier. There was nothing, though, neither sound nor light nor movement, and Ronon ventured to switch his own light back on, keeping the beam trained on the ground.

"Wait here."

He eased forward, keeping his light low. Up close, it was clear that the miners had dragged a damaged hand-cart sideways across the rails, and then piled rocks and broken timbers on and around it until the passage was blocked. There were no lights beyond the barrier, no signs that it was being watched, and he risked letting his light play over the heaped wreckage. It didn't completely fill the tunnel, but it would take time and effort to dismantle it enough to get past. "Is there another way around?"

Kos bent over her maps. "I'm not finding one. It looks as though this is the only passage between the new and old mines."

Pin edged closer, and when Ronon didn't wave him away, turned his own light on the barrier. "This — it wouldn't be that hard to take this down," he said, after a moment. "So why aren't they guarding it?"

"Because there haven't been any Wraith in years?" Bar said. She added her light to the others. "Can't we just pull out a few pieces? Climb through that way?"

"Maybe," Pin said, and Tec shrugged.

Ronon took a step back, considering the pile. It was lower on the left, as though the builders had run out of suitable debris before they quite finished. If you pulled down those two big pieces of wood, that would free the chunk of rock. It would be heavy, but not impossible to lever free… And then he saw it, just a flick of light in the beam of his head lamp, a glint of wire among the debris. "Hold it."

The others froze, and Ronon moved closer, aiming his light into the tangle. It was a wire, all right, rusted and blackened but held taut between the wall and something in the debris. He let the light follow the wire all the way to the tunnel wall, to see a small ceramic knob set into the stone. "Trip wire."

Someone swore, and Pin edged forward. "Electrified?"

"Yeah." Ronon turned his attention to the other end of the wire. "Yeah, it looks like there's a battery here. Behind that piece of rock."

"I see it," Pin said. "I wonder — if I were building this, I'd design it to set off an alarm somewhere. That way, if the Wraith came through, you'd have plenty of advance warning."

Ronon nodded. "Can you disable it without setting off the alarm?"

"Maybe?" Pin shook his head. "I'll give it a try."

In the end, it took all of them to lever away the two big chunks of railroad tie, and heave the stone inward into the tunnel ahead of them. Ronon winced at the noise, but nothing stirred, and after a minute he nodded to Pin. "Ok."

Pin returned the nod, and began very carefully to free the battery from the rocks around it. Once he had it clear, he moved it slowly away, careful to keep the wire taut, and set it on the ground away from the barrier. "I don't think it's rigged to give off a shock," he said. "So that's one good thing. But I'm worried that cutting it might close a deadman switch and set off the alarm."

"If it's not electrified," Tec began, and Ronon nodded.

"Leave it. Their attention should be on Major Lorne up at the entrance." With luck, he added silently, but there was no point in discouraging his people. "Let's clear the rest of this, and then we can keep going."

***

The maps said they were well into the original part of the mine, and for the first time Ronon could see signs of recent occupation. They passed several chambers that were clearly being used as trash dumps, and it was obvious that the electrical cables that ran along the tunnel walls had been replaced since the mine was closed. There were footprints, too, not new, but certainly obvious, a scuffed path in the dust, and Ronon waved for the group to halt.

"Ok," he said, to Kos. "Where are we now?"

She held out the folded paper, and Pin obligingly slanted a flashlight beam so that it illuminated only the paper. "We're here, on the main level. This is what they used to call the Eastern Line. It runs into the Gallery, here — that's where most of the smaller tunnels meet."

"They loaded the ore cars there," Tec said. He glanced at the rails running down the center of the tunnel. "I don't think they're doing that now —"

"But they might be using them further on," Ronon said. If he was living this deep inside a mountain, he'd want a more reliable method of hauling supplies than packing them in one miner at a time. Even the old pump-handle platform cars would be more efficient than that. "All right. Lights out, except for shaded flashlights. Single file. Let's go."

They made their way cautiously down the corridor, which pitched up slightly as they approached the gallery. Ronon moved as quietly as he could manage, setting his feet carefully on the shifting debris. Ahead, the darkness seemed to grow fainter, as though there were a light some distance ahead, and he lifted his hand to stop the others. "Wait here. I'm going ahead."

He crept forward without waiting for their response, crouching and pulling close to the wall as the light brightened. Yes, there were lights ahead, electric bulbs suspended from the ceiling; they ran down three of the corridors that led west toward the entrance. He paused for a long moment, stilling his breath to listen, but there was no sound from any of the corridors. When he edged close enough to peer into the nearest opening, there was nothing but stone and shadow as far as he could see. The others were the same, and he flashed his light once, signaling the others to join him.

"I think we've reached the edge of where they're living," he said softly. "Do we risk the lighted areas, or is there a way around?"

"It depends on where we're going," Kos said. She shook her head. "And honestly I haven't the faintest idea where they might hold prisoners."

"Do you think the doctor has found anything?" Tec asked.

Ronon suppressed the desire to point out that they knew exactly as much as he did about that. "Move back. I'm going to try to contact him."

They moved back into the shadows until they were — he hoped — out of earshot of anyone approaching from the connecting tunnels, and Ronon reached for his radio. Before he could begin transmitting, however, Bar said nervously, "Wait, did you hear that?"

"Quiet," Ronon hissed, and flicked off his flashlight. The others did the same, and in the thick dark, they could all hear it, the sound of something heavy bumping over the stone floor. There were voices with it, a murmur of conversation. He risked a glance around the edge of the opening, and saw two shapes moving against the light, dragging a wooden sledge behind them. From the shape of it, it was piled with garbage, and he bit back a curse. "Everybody. Into the left-hand tunnel, flatten yourselves against the wall." It wouldn't be much cover, but it would be better than nothing, particularly since the miners were coming out of relative brightness into the dark of the gallery.

He heard scuffling as the others obeyed, and winced, risking another glance to see if the miners had heard. They were coming on, apparently oblivious, and he could make out their words now.

"— think the general's right?"

That was a woman's voice, or a boy's; a woman's, he guessed, from how calm it sounded.

"He says they're Wraith worshippers," a man answered, sounding doubtful. "But I don't know."

"I got a look at their equipment," the woman said. "It's not Wraith. And not Genii, either."

"You don't think — the stories about Atlantis can't be true." They were getting closer, the sledge thumping awkwardly along the rails. "I mean, they can't. People from another galaxy? Heirs of the Ancestors? Come on."

"Why not people from another galaxy?" the woman

retorted. "And if they're enemies of the Wraith, we ought to be talking to them."

"Well. That's the question, isn't it? Why would the general lie?"

"I don't know," the woman answered, "but he's done it before."

"That was different," the man said.

There was a silence, broken by the ever-increasing noise of the sledge scraping along the rails, and then the woman said, "My cousin saw the aircraft. Nobody's ever seen anything like it. It's not Genii, it's not Hoffan, it's not Wraith. I think they're what they say they are."

"So what do you suggest we do about it?" the man asked. They were almost at the tunnel entrance, their shadows falling ahead of them.

"We elected him," the woman said. "We can unelect him."

"He's a general," the man said, with a short laugh. "He's got the guns."

"Yes, but there's only one of him."

"Plus the half of us who think he's a great guy."

"I don't want us shooting each other," the woman said. "But — something is just not right."

Ronon took a deep breath. If Teyla were here, she'd step out of the shadows, hands open and empty, give them that trader's smile of hers and walk away with new allies. And maybe that was the way to play this. He couldn't exactly fight his way in, not with only four people for back-up, and if they did get in and rescue Hocken and Tan, the odds of getting out without a fight were slim to none. But if some of the miners already doubted the general's story, maybe he could convince them. He flicked his weapon's setting to stun, and stepped out into the fan of light spilling out of the tunnel.

"Don't run." He winced — that was probably not the best

way to start the conversation — and added, "I'm not going to hurt you."

The man reached for his rifle, and Ronon lifted his own weapon in answer.

"Wait," the woman said. "He's — you're one of them. One of the Lanteans."

"I'm Satedan," Ronon said. "And I'm working with Atlantis. We just want to get our people back."

He could hear the rest of his party moving up behind him, and the woman gave them a sharp look.

"You — are you Satedan, too?"

"We are," Kos said.

"We're coming back," Ronon said. "Rebuilding in the capital. The governor sent Hocken and Tan to look for survivors, only their plane had problems. We don't want to hurt anybody or cause you any more problems than you've already got. But we're not leaving them here."

The miners exchanged a look, and then the man said, "What about the Wraith?"

"They've got problems of their own," Ronon said. This was not the time to go into the details of Lantean policy, or how doubtful he still was that it would work. "And the Lanteans have weapons that will kill them. Permanently. That's why we've allied with them."

"Weapons that will kill Wraith," the man repeated, and the woman said, not quite under her breath, "I knew this wasn't making sense."

"We just want to get our people out safely," Ronon said. "Can you help us?"

They exchanged another look, and then the man nodded, sighing. The woman said, "I know where they're keeping them. But you need to talk to Erkesen Tas first. He'll help you —"

Ronon shook his head. "Take us to our people first. Then — I'll talk to him if I can."

***

Radek made his way along the corridor, trying to walk as though he belonged there. Not that it would help if anyone got a good look at him, the miners' community was small enough that they would know everyone by sight, but from a distance he should pass for a miner. And surely he didn't have much further to go. Ahead of him, he could see the pair who had been sent from the communal kitchen, the woman carrying a heavy tray, the man carrying a basket and what looked like a shotgun tucked under his arm. They had to be taking food to their prisoners, and from what he remembered of the map, they were reaching the end of the diggings on this side.

Sure enough, the ground began to slope downward under his feet, and he could see a new light ahead as the tunnel widened. He could hear voices, too, and cocked his head to listen, but couldn't distinguish Hocken's voice among the others. And of course that was an unforeseen problem — what if the general had more than one group of prisoners, more than one set of cells? — but there was only one way to deal with that. He glanced around quickly, finding yet another of the little alcoves that lined the tunnels. He risked a quick exploration with his flashlight, and saw with relief that it was deep enough to conceal him completely. There was still no one behind him, and he eased forward until he could see into the tunnel's end.

There were cells, all right, practical jail cells cut into the rock, with barred doors that looked discouragingly solid. Still, the locks were large and looked old-fashioned, and surely a little C4 would knock them loose — and bring the rest of the miners running, he reminded himself. That would be a last resort. The cell to his right held three Satedan men, but

to the left, he could see Hocken and Tan, Hocken leaning
on the bars talking urgently to the woman with the tray. As
he watched, the woman shook her head, turning away, and
Radek darted back to the shelter of the alcove. He flattened
himself against the dank stone and waited, watching as their
head lamps grew brighter in the corridor.

"— shouldn't have to take care of Wraith worshippers,"
the woman said, and the man made what sounded like a
noise of protest.

"Maybe they're not."

"The general says so," the woman answered, and then
they were past.

Radek waited until their light and the sound of their footsteps had receded down the tunnel, the reached for his radio.
Best to let someone know where the prisoners were being held
in case something went wrong.

"Ronon, this is Zelenka." He kept his voice just above a
whisper, but even so winced at the sound. "Come in, Ronon."
There was a long silence, only static hissing in his earpiece,
and he tried again. "Ronon, this is Zelenka. Please come in."

"Ronon here. What's your position?"

Radek let out a breath. "I've found Hocken and Tan." He
glanced quickly at his tablet. "Map 4.1, grid B-8, at the end
of the longest tunnel."

"Copy that," Ronon said. There was a pause, as though
he was checking something. "Can you get them out? We're
coming to you."

Yes, with explosives, but — Radek swallowed the words.
"Yes."

"Right." There was another pause, not as long this time,
and then Ronon's voice came briskly. "We'll rendezvous at
the intersection at the edge of Map 5.2, that's on the same line,
but down one level. If we get there first, we'll keep coming.

If you get there first, wait for us."

"Yes," Radek said, and then, remembering, "Yes, roger, I copy that."

"See you there," Ronon said, and broke the connection.

Radek slipped out of the alcove again. The cell area was lit by a single electric bulb in the ceiling, and there was no sign of a security camera. But of course the Satedans hadn't achieved that level of technology, he reminded himself, and stepped into view.

"Colonel Hocken."

"Dr. Zelenka!" She managed to keep her voice down, but the men in the other cell called out, demanding to know what was going on, and Radek waved frantically at them.

"Will you be quiet? Someone will hear."

That shut them up, and Radek turned his attention to the lock on the cell door. Certainly a little C4 would do the job, and probably not bring down the roof, but there had to be a quieter way to deal with it.

"Where's — who else is here?" Hocken wrapped her hands around the bars as though she was trying to see further down the tunnel.

"Major Lorne is at the front gate," Radek said. He unfolded his multi-tool, selecting a screwdriver bit to probe the enormous keyhole. He could feel the wards, but couldn't quite make them move. "Ronon is bringing people to meet us."

"You have to take us with you," one of the men said. "You have to!"

"Should we?" Radek looked at Hocken, who shrugged.

"Yeah, I think we have to. Mar — General Mar, he's the guy who's behind all of this — he hired them to carry supplies to the mine, told them it was an exploring expedition."

"Except we weren't exploring," a fair-haired young man said. "He knew perfectly well where we were going. He told us if we'd keep our mouths shut when we got back to the capital, he'd share the profits —"

"Only Atil here isn't real good at keeping his mouth shut," the other young man said. "We didn't say yes fast enough, so he called us Wraith worshippers, and they locked us up in here."

"He was never going to let us go," the oldest of the three said bitterly. "Don't kid yourself."

"If we don't bring them with us," Tan said, "he'll try to use them against us."

"Yes," Radek said. He couldn't pick the lock, but perhaps — yes, the screws were on the outside of the lock, not easily accessible to a prisoner, and you'd need a screwdriver anyway, but — that he had. He found the correct bit and turned hard. The metal groaned, and gave way under the pressure. "Yes, that's good. You said profits? What is he after, the general?"

Hocken shrugged. "This was a silver mine. Silver, maybe?"

"You'd have to take a lot of it to make it worthwhile," Radek said, still working at the screws. "And surely you'd have to take it off world to sell it?"

"It's not silver," the oldest man said. "It's a black rock, heavy for its size. Kind of oily looking."

"Come on, Yori, that can't be it," the blond man said.

"It's ore of some kind," the other man said.

One of the screws came free at last. Radek tucked it into his pocket and started on the next one. "Did they give it a name?"

"Pitch," the oldest man said. "Pitch-something. I remember because I thought he was going to burn it."

Radek froze, a memory flooding back: his first year at university, a near-empty classroom on an unseasonably warm day, the windows open to let in the smell of blooming trees. The professor passing chunks of rock around the classroom, daring them to guess what they were… He remembered one piece, about the size of his fist, almost black, with an odd, oiled sheen to its surface. "Pitchblende. Was that what he called it?"

The older man shrugged. "Maybe?"

Pitchblende. Uraninite. It took all his willpower to keep his hands steady on the multitool, winding a second screw out of its place. A radioactive ore of uranium, often found in lead and silver mines. One made nuclear fuels from it, and plutonium for bombs. He remembered the way everyone had moved away when the professor told them what it was, the shiver that had run down his own spine when the professor waved the wand of a Geiger counter over it, producing a grating screech.

From the look on Hocken's face, she recognized the name as well. "Pitchblende. Isn't that —"

"A radioactive ore," Radek said grimly, and fed another screw. He looked at the Satedans. "It gives off some of the same energies you use for x-rays."

The three men exchanged glances. "Is it dangerous?"

Radek started on the next screw, grunting as he threw his weight against it. "It can be. If you're exposed to it for long periods of time, it can make you sick."

There was a little silence, and then Tan said what they were all thinking. "The miners — they've been living down here since the Wraith attacked."

"You have to be close to it to be affected," Radek said, but he thought she was right to worry. The lock's face plate came free at last, and he chose a thick bit to work the latch. The door swung back, and Hocken quickly caught it before it could close again.

"You've got unexpected talents, Doc. Thanks."

"Spend enough time on Atlantis, and you will learn the most unlikely things." Radek turned his attention to the other cell. Having done it once, it was easier to get the second door opened, and the men came hurrying out. In the better light, the blond looked familiar, and Radek frowned. "Do you have a sister? Valiena Bar?"

"Yes!" The young man looked startled and pleased at the same time. "Yes, I'm Atil…"

"She has been worried about you," Radek said. "She was with our group, probably with Ronon."

"We should get moving," Hocken said.

"Yes — yes, you're right." Radek returned the multi-tool to his pocket. "Ronon should be waiting."

***

Ronon followed the two miners down the corridor, aware of his own people following almost silently. There were no ceiling lights here, just their own head lamps, and the walls looked oddly damp in places, as though water was seeping from some hidden seam. They were a level below the area being used as cells, or so the woman had said, pointing out their track on the maps he'd shown her by the light of his shaded head lamp. She had introduced herself as Theanna Nen, and the man as Merivik Kei; he had been a miner, Ronon gathered, and she had worked as a dentist's assistant in one of the supply towns at the base of the Spur. She had been visiting a cousin when the Wraith attacked, and had stayed to help with her children. Two years ago, she had walked most of the way down the Spur, but the town where she had lived was ash and empty ruin, trees sprouting through the wreck of the dentist's office.

"I do wonder what happened to them," she had confided, when they had stopped to rest and wolf down protein bars, "if any of them made it off-world — so I pretend they did, and imagine they're living happily on Manara or Kappes or someplace like that."

They were almost certainly dead, the dentist and her

friends and her brother who had lived in the capital, but Ronon knew she understood that as well as he did. And he had discovered that some of his friends had survived, though that had not been a good thing in the end. "Anything's possible," he had said, and they had moved on.

He was angrier than he had expected, angry at Mar for lying, not just because it trapped these people in the depths of a mine where humans were never meant to live, but because it denied everything Cai had been trying to do. The returned Satedans had done so much, rebuilding the area around the Stargate, driving off the Genii, setting up new trade agreements that would let them do even more. It was wrong to deny them that possibility, particularly when Mar knew perfectly well what was happening. It was a calculated cruelty that made him want to pound Mar's head against a stone wall.

It also made no sense. Why didn't Mar want the miners to know about the new settlement in the capital? It wasn't as though many of these people were going to make the long walk out of the mountains. It wouldn't have cost Mar anything, one iota of his power, to say that people had come back to the capital, but that it wasn't safe to trade with them. There wasn't any need for this complicated story about Wraith worshippers and Atlantis as a hoax. At least not that he could see. He scowled, frustrated, the beam of his head lamp sweeping across more dark, oily stone. Teyla would have figured it out by now. That was exactly the sort of thing she was good at, listening and smiling, until she had all the pieces in her hands and could reveal them like the winning cards in a game of wild nines. Sheppard would have gotten it, too, with his questions that never seemed to quite aim at his target, but always got there in the end. Whereas he himself... he didn't know what to ask, or how to ask without upsetting the fragile balance. The main thing was to rescue Hocken and Tan, he told himself firmly. Get them out, make sure they're not in any danger, and we can worry about the rest later. And rescuing them was something he could do.

They had reached a spot where the tunnel widened into a circular chamber, and three more tunnels came in at angles. A single flickering bulb hung from the center of the ceiling, and the woman Nen raised a finger to signal silence. Ronon nodded, and stopped beside her before he spoke, keeping his voice low.

"Problem?"

"We're here," Kei said, equally softly. He pointed to the nearest of the new entrances. "That's a spiral ramp, leads up to the main level. It comes out at the head of the corridor that leads down to the cells."

"Right." It looked faintly lighter inside the spiral, and Ronon flicked off his head-lamp. "Ok. I'm on point. Nen, you're with me. The rest of you, stay here. If there's any trouble, don't try to help, just fade out and get back to Lorne. Got that?"

There was a murmur of agreement, and Wood said, "Yes, sir."

Ronon looked at Nen. "Let's go."

The ramp wound upward in a tight spiral, steep enough that Ronon wouldn't have liked to try to get a handcart down those slopes. He said as much to Nen, who shook her head.

"This is for personnel. Equipment goes on the lifts."

Ronon nodded, remembering the marks on the maps. "Are they still running?"

"Some of them. We're short of rope and cable."

"We could trade for that," Ronon said. "We've salvaged some in the capital."

Nen gave him a sidelong look, her expression unreadable in the dim light. "This — you've really gotten that far? And the Wraith haven't come back?"

"They've been fighting a war of their own," Ronon answered, and couldn't keep a certain satisfaction from his voice. "And we're allied with Atlantis. The Wraith don't want to mess with them."

"I don't understand," Nen said. "Why wouldn't the general —"

Something moved in the shadows ahead of them, and Ronon held up his hand. Nen froze, then flattened herself against the wall beside him. He cocked his head, listening, then slid forward so that he could see around the next curve. They were almost at the top of the ramp, thin light shining down from the bulbs that ran along the walls of the upper corridor, and he could hear soft voices just outside the entrance. He motioned for Nen to stay still, and edged forward, his weapon ready, moving as softly as he could on the gravel-strewn ground. The lights from the corridor spilled into the opening, but the curve of the ramp left enough of a shadow for him to hide in. He rested his back against the damp stone and eased himself toward the entrance. The voices were louder now, though he still couldn't make out the words: several people, men and women, talking quickly and quietly, voices tight with tension. Had the miners discovered the escape already? He leaned forward, and let out his breath in a huge sigh of relief as he spotted Zelenka and Hocken among the group.

"Hey," he said, keeping his voice low.

The group whirled to face him, Hocken with a P90 ready — Zelenka's, Ronon guessed. Zelenka had a pistol, and the others, Tan and three strangers, lifted heavy sticks that looked as though they'd been scavenged from the mine itself. Zelenka recognized him first, sagging with relief, and Hocken dropped the muzzle of her weapon.

"Ronon! Are we glad to see you!"

"Everybody all right?" They all seemed uninjured, but Ronon was still relieved when Hocken nodded.

"Yeah. We're good. We just need to get out of here."

Ronon leaned back into the mouth of the ramp, waved for Nen to come forward. "Yeah. What's our best way to get back to the main entrance?"

"The general's going to have that blocked," Nen answered.

"Are there any other exits on this side of the Spur?" Ronon checked the corridor around them. No sign of pursuit, but that wouldn't last forever.

"I don't think so?" Nen spread her hands. "I'm not a miner, though."

Ronon looked at the other Satedans who had been locked up with Hocken and Tan, but they shook their heads. He closed his eyes, trying to remember the maps. They wouldn't be any worse off if they went down one level, and that might confuse anyone looking for them. "Right. This way. Nen, you lead."

She obeyed without hesitation, starting back down the tight spiral, and Ronon fell into step between Hocken and Zelenka.

"Who are these guys?"

"General Mar hired them to carry supplies up to the mine," Hocken said. "Only then he wanted them to go along with some story about Wraith worshippers, and they weren't quick enough to say yes, so he locked them up."

"One of them is Valiena Bar's missing brother," Zelenka said.

Ronon nodded. "Good. Do you have any idea what Mar is after? Because none of this is making a lot of sense."

"Not so much." Zelenka sounded grim. "They are mining pitchblende, uranium ore, but I don't know what he wants it for."

"And this is a problem." Ronon made the words a statement rather than a question, and Zelenka shrugged.

"Pitchblende — uranium dioxide — is radioactive. We use it on Earth to make uranium for nuclear fission, fuel for power plants and bombs." Zelenka shook his head. "It's dangerous to be too close to it for long periods of time. The Genii found that out. But Sateda doesn't have any use for radioactive materials, your technology hasn't advanced that far. Though — you had radium, I think, before the Wraith?"

"We had x-ray machines," Ronon said.

Zelenka nodded. "But for that you need radium, smaller sources than you could process from the material from this mine, or it would have been a good deal more profitable in its day."

"But why does he want uranium?" Hocken said. "Nobody here —"

She stopped abruptly, and Ronon said, "The Genii. They're still trying to make those bombs. And this would be a big step, right?"

"Maybe," Zelenka said. "It has to be processed, refined — you can't just walk out of here with a few lumps of ore and expect to make a weapon." He sighed. "But if that's not it… No, I don't know."

Ronon shook his head. The Genii had their Ancient spacecraft, even if it had been pretty badly shot up. It wasn't impossible to imagine them landing here without Cai knowing. But the Lanteans would know, and Radim, at least, seemed to want to keep on their good side for now. Though if Mar had showed up in the capital with a wagon-load of rocks and said he knew somewhere he could trade for them, no one would have stopped him, either. He put the thought aside as they reached the bottom of the spiral.

"Atil!" Valiena Bar managed to keep her voice down as the party emerged from the spiral, but flung herself at her brother. He caught her, looking at once grateful and embarrassed as she wound her arms around him. "You never checked in. I've been so worried!"

"I'm fine, Val, really."

"Save it for later," Ronon said. "We need to get out of here, preferably without having to walk back through the mine." The thought of trying to thread their way back out through the maze of tunnels made him break out in a cold sweat. "Does anybody know a way out on this side?"

The miners exchanged another look, and Kei said, "I don't. But Erseken Tas will."

"He's not been happy with the general," Nen said. "He'll help you."

Ronon hesitated, but it was the best option he had. "All right. Take us to him."

CHAPTER SIX

NEN LED them quickly through the darkened tunnels, stopping at last at the foot of another spiral ramp. "Wait here."

"No." Ronon caught her sleeve before she could get away. "I'll go with you."

"Can you trust her?" Zelenka asked.

Nen glared at him. "I've brought you this far —"

They had to trust her, Ronon thought. She had to be trustworthy, or there was no way they were going to win the miners back to being Satedans again. But that was too complicated to explain right now, and there wasn't time. "We have to," he said, and pointed to Kei. "You stay here. Hocken, if I'm not back in half an hour, find a way out on your own."

"Will do." Hocken's hands closed tight on the butt of the P90, then opened again. They both knew there wasn't much chance of getting out without help, but there was nothing else to do.

"Ok," Ronon said, and looked at Nen. "Lead on."

She led him through a tangle of narrow corridors that had obviously been converted from active mining to living space. The lights were brighter here, the bulbs hanging at shorter intervals, and in spots boards had been set up against the walls to hide the stone. It was warmer, too, the air less damp, and there were more people visible in the halls. Nen tried to keep to the least crowded tunnels, but even so Ronon kept his head down and hoped no one was paying close attention.

At last they stopped at a door that had been set into an arched opening in the tunnel wall. The wood had been painted a vivid, spring-leaf green, and what looked like a cowbell without a clapper hung in the center of the boards. Nen tapped gently on it, and a moment later the door opened and a dark-skinned woman peered out, her greying braids caught up in a strip of bright red fabric.

"Theanna?"

"I need to talk to Erkesen right now," Nen said.

"He's really busy," the dark woman began, and then her eyes widened as she saw Ronon.

"It's urgent," Nen said, and the dark woman nodded, pulling the door open.

"So I see."

The door gave onto a room that might have come from one of the magazines Melena had read before the Wraith came, paneled walls painted white to reflect the lamplight, an electric mountain stove with bars glowing orange and an iron kettle steaming on the hob, a trestle table and wooden stools and even a cushioned armchair. A basket beside it held carded wool and a spindle half-full of spun thread, and an embroidered curtain covered a doorway that had to lead to inner rooms. Before Ronon could say anything, the curtain was swept aside, and a tall man ducked under its curve, only to stop abruptly, seeing a stranger.

"Father says —"

"They want to talk to Erkesen," the woman said, with a wry smile. "I think they should."

The tall man — he had the woman's mouth, Ronon thought, was probably her son — gave her a startled look, then blinked as he focused on Ronon. "Yeah. I guess so."

He stepped back, still holding the curtain, and Ronon followed Nen into the second room. The woman came in after them, her feet silent on the well-swept floor. "Father."

An older man, his steel-gray hair cut close to his scalp, looked up from his place at the head of a long table. This was obviously the room that served as a work room, with a long table beneath the cluster of lights, and a curtained bed tucked into one corner. Another curtain covered a doorway that led further into the mountain: a bedroom, Ronon guessed.

"What's this?" The older man stopped abruptly. "I suppose I should say 'who.'"

"He's from Atlantis," Nen said. "Like the others."

"I'm Satedan," Ronon said. It was suddenly important to make that clear. "Ronon Dex. I was a Technical Specialist under Kell when the Wraith came. But, yeah, I work with the Lanteans now."

"Mar says Atlantis is a Wraith trick." Tas stopped again, shaking his head. "I'm Erkesen Tas. My wife Dreshka Sur, and my son Arton. Theanna I know."

"It's not a trick," Ronon said. Tas gestured to a chair, and Ronon seated himself, though the muscles down his spine crawled at the thought of making himself that vulnerable. Arton brought a teapot and cups and filled them, while Sur took a seat at her husband's side. "I've been — I've lived on Atlantis. They're exactly what they say they are, travelers from another galaxy, and they'll stand up with us against the Wraith." He believed that, he realized. They were trying to get out of it, because, sentimentally or foolishly or just out of inability to believe that that Wraith were what they were, they thought the Wraith could be saved. But when it came to a choice, they would fight beside their fellow humans.

"Strangers from another galaxy," Tas said. "What did they come here for? And why did they pick you?"

"They came to explore," Ronon said. "And they didn't pick me. I —" He stopped, frustrated, fumbling for the words that would explain why he'd thrown in his lot with Atlantis when there had seemed to be nothing either to gain or lose. "I told you, I was a Technical Specialist when the Wraith attacked. That was in the capital. We fought as long as we could —" And that was a memory he refused to face, not today, and he stumbled on. "But finally I was taken. And when I woke up, a Wraith told me I'd been chosen. I was to be a Runner. They'd give me a head start and if I could get to the Stargate, I could run. Because they wanted the fun of hunting me down."

He glared at Tas, daring him to disbelieve, but the miner nodded. "I've heard — we've all heard of such things."

"So I ran," Ronon said. "I killed the first Wraith and took his weapon and made it through the gate. After that — I kept running. They kept chasing. Seven years in, I ran into a Lantean scouting party." He stopped again, the events still defying belief. "I took a couple of them hostage, so I could get out through the gate. They offered to have their surgeon remove the tracker the Wraith had put in my back, and find out what had happened on Sateda since I was taken. They kept their word. They were living in the city of the Ancestors, using its technology to fight the Wraith and to help people where they could, and — Sateda was destroyed, then. I threw in my lot with them. Joined a team. And when they brought Atlantis back, I came with them, and we found that people had started coming back to Sateda. I've been acting as, I guess, a liaison since then." He shrugged. "The Wraith were massing for a war of their own, and we fought them, beat them back for now."

He stopped then, the thing that he didn't want to have to admit on the tip of his tongue. Atlantis had destroyed Queen Death, yes, but they had made a bargain with other Wraith to do so.

"How could they possibly…" Sur's voice trailed off.

Ronon took a deep breath. He couldn't lie, not even by omission, not if he wanted the miners to trust him. Though if they would trust him afterward — he shoved that thought away. "One Wraith queen was trying to control all the Wraith, and we ended up fighting alongside a faction that opposed her. Once Death was dead, the Lanteans made a truce: the Wraith agreed to stay out of our part of the galaxy, and the Lanteans agreed not to pursue them into theirs."

He could feel the cold disbelief spreading through the room, even Nen pulling away from him a little. Arton said, "What about the people in the Wraith part of the galaxy? Are the Lanteans just leaving them there?"

"There's a new drug," Ronon said. "A retrovirus. It lets the Wraith feed on people without killing them."

"That's not enough," Sur said, and Arton shook his head. "Is that what the general meant? That Atlantis made a deal with the Wraith?"

In the same moment, Tas said, "They're mad. What makes them think the Wraith will keep their word? They're just buying time until they can attack again."

"I think you're right," Ronon said. "We can't trust them. But this buys us time, too. By the time the Wraith break the truce, we'll be ready to fight back, more than we ever were before. And the Lanteans will fight beside us."

"You're sure of that?" Tas sounded skeptical, and Ronon put every ounce of conviction he could muster into his answer.

"Yeah. I'm sure." Sheppard and Teyla would be sorry to be proved wrong — it would hurt Teyla badly when the Wraith betrayed her — but he had no doubt at all that they would join the rest of the galaxy to defend humanity. It was a truth he hadn't acknowledged before, and even at this moment he was obscurely warmed by it.

"You work for them anyway," Tas said.

"We disagree. I think they've made a mistake." Ronon took a breath. "But that doesn't make them bad people."

"And you still live on Atlantis," Sur said, into the spreading silence.

"I do, yeah." Ronon nodded. "While they need me. But — probably not forever. I'll come home one day." He hadn't known that until he'd said it, but it felt right, another comfortable, comforting truth.

"You trust them that far," Tas said.

"There wouldn't be a home to come to without Lantean support," Ronon answered.

"If you're not working for Sateda," Arton asked, "why were you up here?"

"Colonel Hocken — she's Lantean herself, but she works for the governor now — she was doing some surveying. We're still looking for survivors," Ronon answered. "I was leading a team that was looking into getting the Narmoth Falls power plant running again when Hocken had engine trouble."

"That explains a lot," Tas said. "I saw the equipment they brought back with the prisoners, and I talked to people who saw the aircraft. It didn't sound like anything the Wraith would make."

"I don't know what General Mar wants from you," Ronon said, "and right now I'm not in a place to help you figure that out. But if you'll help me get my people out of here, we'll help you deal with him."

"We don't know what he wants either," Tas said. "He's lied to us for years, and I have no idea why. So, yes, we'll help you, and then, yes, I'll be glad of your help to figure out what to do next."

"It's a deal," Ronon said, and they shook hands across the table.

***

When the miners returned, they returned in force, not just Ronon and Nen but a dozen people led by a graying man whom Ronon introduced as Erkesen Tas. Radek dragged himself to his feet to be introduced, tiredly amazed that Hocken still seemed fully alert and functional, and made himself listen to the plan.

"— make our way to the gallery," Tas was saying, "get out through the old lift window."

"That hasn't been opened in twenty years," someone protested.

"We're just going to let them go?" That was Kei, stepping out from among the Satedans who had come with Ronon. There was no way to tell one group from the other, Radek thought, which would work to their advantage if there was a problem. It was just a pity that the Atlantis team stuck out like sore thumbs. "They said they'd help us with the general, well, they ought to help us! Not run off and leave us to deal with him."

"It's an earnest of our good intentions," Tas said. "They don't know which of us kidnapped their people."

"And I'll be staying with you," Ronon said. "On behalf of Atlantis and the provisional government."

Radek gave him a sharp look at that, ready to protest, but swallowed the words. Ronon was right, that was a fair exchange for help escaping. Hocken looked as though she was making the same reluctant decision. "Ok," she said, "but we'd better get a move on. They're going to find out any second now that we're loose."

"Agreed," Tas said. "Vassi, what's the general doing?"

"The last time I checked, still yelling out the front gate." That was a thin girl with her hair pulled back in a double pony tail. "The Lanteans were talking nice, though."

As they would, Radek thought. Lorne wasn't going to risk the captives. And by now, they'd probably brought in reinforcements, more Marines and even Sheppard himself.

"Right." Tas gathered his people with a gesture. "Let's go."

They made their way through a series of tunnels that seemed to Radek's tired eyes nearly identical to all the other tunnels he had been through. At one point, he thought they were going down, and then they crossed to another, wider tunnel that sloped steeply upward. He reached again for his tablet, trying to keep track of where they were, and one of the Satedans hissed at him.

"Hey. Put that away, someone will see."

She was right, of course, and Radek obeyed, but he hated the feeling he was running blind. Hocken gave him a wary look, his P90 still clutched to her chest.

"I guess you don't have any idea where we are?"

Radek shook his head. "I could find us if I had to," he said, and hoped it was true.

There was a flurry of movement at the head of the column, and a confused and muffled noise that traveled back along the group and resolved into whispers of "Hold it! Stay still!" Radek froze, gripping his pistol tightly, and hoped he wouldn't have to use it. A meter or so ahead of him, he saw Tan adjust her grip on the staff she carried as an improvised weapon, and Hocken slipped off the safety on her P90.

"What is it?" he whispered, and Tan shook her head.

"The way's blocked? I don't know…"

And then there was more movement behind them, shouts and stumbling, bodies jostling into him. He whirled, holding the pistol high, and saw another group moving toward them, more of the heavy staffs in their hands, lowered like spears.

"This way!" someone shouted, and Radek turned with the crowd, fighting blindly down a too-narrow tunnel. And then there was light ahead, and the tunnel opened abruptly into the mine's broad entrance. A group of armed men turned to face them, and Tas yelled, "Go, go, go!"

He and his armed men charged forward, trying to overwhelm the general's group by sheer weight of numbers, but only a handful of them had rifles. Radek saw Ronon firing bolt after bolt, but the charge faltered, people dropping back into the shelter of overturned carts and mining equipment.

"Back here!" Hocken yelled, and fired a burst from the P90. She aimed high, the shots chipping stones from the arch and Radek saw the men at the head of the tunnel flinch and duck back into its shelter. "Zelenka! Ammo?"

Radek fumbled in his pockets, came up with the spare magazines and passed them over, then reached for his radio. "Major Lorne, this is Zelenka. Major Lorne, come in."

The response was reassuringly prompt. "Doc! What's going on in there?"

"We're in the entrance area," Radek answered, "caught between two of the general's teams —"

"Hang in there." That was Sheppard, no surprise. "We're coming to you."

"Understood —" Radek began, and Ronon's voice crackled in his earpiece.

"We're halfway down the hall from the entrance, anything in front of you is hostile."

"Copy that," Sheppard said, and a moment later there was a bang and a great flash of light from just inside the entrance. Radek ducked, swearing, his eyes tearing from the blast, and there was another flurry of shots from the general's men, as though they were firing blind at the source of the sounds. Radek swore again, searching for a target, but it was hard to tell friend from enemy in the shifting light. The miners were all dressed alike, armed alike, and he shook his head in frustration. Behind him, Hocken fired again, bullets chattering off stone, and Radek flinched, thinking of ricochets.

"Hold it!" The shout came from the center of the fighting, and Radek turned to see a confusion of shadows resolve to the general with one arm crooked around the neck of a dark young man, his other hand holding a pistol to the young man's head. "Erkesen, I don't want to hurt him, but I'll kill him if you don't call off your men."

"Hold your fire!" Tas shouted. "Evrast, you can't keep this up. You've been lying to us all this time —"

Radek reached for his radio, spoke quietly into the mic. "Colonel Sheppard. We now have a hostage situation."

"Copy that," Sheppard said. "I see it. Lorne, anything you can do?"

"Nothing." Lorne's frustration was clearly audible. "Too long a shot, and we don't have sharpshooters with us anyway."

"Stand by," Sheppard said grimly.

"Lying?" Mar managed a laugh. "Ok, maybe I exaggerated a little, but Atlantis is not our friend."

"You lied to us," Tas said, "lied about who was in the capital. Satedans are coming home, they're rebuilding, and you lied to us about it."

"They've allied with Atlantis," Mar said again. "And Atlantis has made a deal with the Wraith. Oh, I bet they didn't tell you that little detail, did they? They've sold half the galaxy to the Wraith, and it's just luck we're on the human side of that line —"

"I told him that," Ronon said. He stepped out from behind the cover of an overturned ore car, his weapon leveled. "And I told him why."

"It's crazy — we'll all end up dead," Mar answered.

"I believe him," Tas said. "And whether they're wrong or not — that doesn't matter right now. Your stories — they never quite added up, and now we know why."

Mar tightened his grip on the young man's neck. "Call off your people, and call off Atlantis, or I'll shoot him here and now."

"Shoot him, and you'll never walk out of here," another voice said, and Tas lifted his hand.

"She's right, Evrast. Let my son go, and we can talk."

"No." Mar's hand didn't waver on the pistol. "I want passage to the Stargate — the Lanteans can bring me there in one of their aircraft, you can arrange that. And then through the gate. After that, I'll send Arton back."

Radek saw Ronon take a slow step sideways, and then another, angling for a better shot at Mar. With the weapon set to stun, he didn't have to worry about hitting Arton, but even so, it wasn't going to be easy. And it all depended on Mar's attention being elsewhere.

"I don't know what the Lanteans can do," Tas protested. "I don't have any way to talk to them."

Mar hesitated, and Radek took a quick step forward before Mar could focus again on Ronon. "I can. I can call them —"

He didn't know what else he would have said, was saved from having to babble on by the sudden crack of Ronon's weapon. Mar and Arton both dropped, the pistol rolling free unfired, and both Ronon and Tas rushed forward, Tas to pull his son away from the general's now-lax grip, Ronon to fire a second shot into Mar's limp body. Only then did he look around.

"Nice distraction, Doc." He put his hand to his ear. "Sheppard. Everything's under control here. We're all right."

"Yes, well." Radek realized his hands were shaking. Carefully, he put the safety back on, then jammed hands and pistol into the pockets of his jacket. "It's better if nobody gets shot."

"He's just stunned," Ronon said, to Tas, who nodded. Arton was already stirring in his arms: obviously Ronon had used the weapon's lightest setting. "They both are, but Mar's going to be out a while longer."

"As far as I'm concerned, that's a matter for the governor," Tas answered. "But obviously we need to talk this out."

Ronon nodded. "But the rest of us —"

"You're free to go," Tas said, loudly, and there was no protest even from Mar's loyalists.

They made their way out into the twilight to find two jumpers parked in the open area in front of the mine's entrance, two squads of Marines unfolding themselves from the positions they'd taken up over the course of the day.

"Nice work," Sheppard said, to Ronon, who shrugged.

"They'll turn Mar over to the governor. I don't know what he can do with him, though."

"That's not our problem, buddy," Sheppard said, and Radek leaned against the side of one of the jumpers, suddenly exhausted.

"I am too old for this," he said, to no one in particular, but Lorne heard, and gave him a wry grin.

"Hocken says they owe you for getting them out of the cells. You sure you don't want to be on a gate team?"

"Very sure," Radek answered, but a certain warmth was spreading through him. He was filthy and tired and wrung out from the aftereffects of fear and adrenaline, but they had come through again.

***

It was sunny and hot when Radek stepped through the Stargate into Sateda's main square, a shock after a day of cold sleet on Atlantis. He nodded to the gate guards — there seemed to be more of them than usual — and then frowned as he realized that Ronon and the governor and half a dozen others were gathered to one side of the square, locked in sober conversation. Hocken was with them, he realized, her hair tied back in a bright Satedan scarf, and as he watched, she broke away from the others to join him.

"Doc! You missed the big event."

"Big event?" Radek frowned. "I came with the new trans-former — sorry, the *modulator* — for the Rapide." He tugged at the strap of his carryall for emphasis.

"The governor just exiled Mar," Hocken said. "They had a trial two days ago, and everyone agreed to strip him of Satedan citizenship and kick him out."

It didn't seem like enough, considering what he'd done, but then, Sateda had no jails, and no people to spare to guard them even if they wanted to turn one of the empty build-ings into a cell. Better to let him go. "That seems reasonable enough," he said cautiously, and Hocken scowled.

"Oh, I understand why they're doing it, but — it's not enough. Keeping those people trapped up in the mine, exposed to radiation —" She shook her head. "That was wrong. Dr. Beckett's offered to send a medical team up there to check on exposures. I'm worried about what he'll find."

"He did manage to keep us safe," a new voice said. Radek blinked, then recognized Dreshka Sur, Erkesen Tas's wife. "During the great culling, and then after. I don't know what changed him, what he wanted, after it was clear there wasn't going to be any more killing, why he decided he had to betray us…"

Her voice trailed off, and Ronon said, "I know."

Radek squinted up at him. "Well? Will you enlighten us?"

Ronon grinned. "He wanted to trade pitchblende to the Genii, for their bombs. He'd heard rumors about them when he was in the capital, and he knew that the Wild Blue produced a source of radium. He figured they could use it."

"That can't be good," Hocken said. "The Genii are the last people I'd trust with nukes."

"I don't think we can stop them," Radek said. "They already know how it's done."

"Yeah, but —" Hocken grimaced. "What do you want to bet he took some pitchblende with him? He's been through the

Stargate a bunch of times, people said, trading stuff he brought down from the mountains. I bet he's got a cache just waiting. And you don't need all that much for what they're doing."

"I hope he did," Cai said. Even Ronon gave him a sideways look at that, and Cai sighed. "The last thing I want is for the Genii to start sniffing around the Wild Blue. They've interfered enough on Sateda."

Ronon nodded. "I'll pass that on to Dr. Weir."

"I'd appreciate that," Cai said. "That was well-handled, Dex." He clapped Ronon on the shoulder, and moved away, turning toward a stocky man who carried a slate note-board and a stick of chalk.

"Yes," Sur said. "We're in your debt."

"I still think he got off too lightly," Hocken said.

Ronon gave her a look. "Lightly?"

"He walked."

"He walked through the gate, yeah," Ronon said slowly, as though he was groping for the right words. "But he left — he left himself behind. He can't call himself Satedan anymore, and the Genii don't accept strangers. Any place he goes, he'll have to say he's not from anywhere. There's no gate address he can dial where they have to take him in." He stopped, shaking his head. "Even when I was a Runner, when Sateda was destroyed and empty, I was still Satedan. He's... nothing."

Radek nodded once, and then again as the words sunk in. It was a bleak vision, and he shook himself hard. "He brought that upon himself. And I have the parts that Colonel Hocken needs to get the Rapide back into good order."

Ronon nodded. "Yeah. Better get to work, then. Who knows what you'll find next time?"

Stay in touch...
Follow us on Twitter
@StargateNovels

Find us on Facebook at
facebook.com/StargateNovels

Sign up for our newsletter
at StargateNovels.com

THANKS!

STARGÅTE
SG·1.

STARGATE
ATLÅNTIS

**Original novels based on the hit
TV shows STARGATE SG-1 and
STARGATE ATLANTIS**

**Available as e-books from leading online
retailers**

**Paperback editions available from
Amazon and IngramSpark**

**If you liked this book, please tell your
friends and leave a review on a
bookstore website. Thanks!**

Made in the USA
Middletown, DE
01 June 2024